PRAISE FOR J <barcode> T0029240

The Poison Flood

"A near-Shakespearean snarl, a mad, seven-day action crucible set in the West Virginia wild . . . *The Poison Flood* is an ambitious saga, cockamamie and passionate. Through Hollis, Farmer produces a pocket Hillbilly manifesto."

—*The Atlanta Journal-Constitution*

"Hollis himself is vivid . . . When the novel focuses on a musician's creative struggles, it sings."

—*Kirkus Reviews*

"Affecting . . . combines an unconventional lead with a sobering portrayal of an environmental disaster's impact on a small community. Readers who like their fiction to have a social conscience will want to take a look."

—*Publishers Weekly*

"[A] bizarre and fascinating read that proves that anything is possible in the capable hands of author Jordan Farmer. The novel is immediately engrossing, its characters uniquely memorable, its prose both heartfelt and stunning. The novel takes a number of unexpected and thrilling turns . . . [and is] rich in compassion and empathy."

—BookPage

"Darkly brilliant and beautifully written . . . [Farmer's] similes, metaphors, and turns of phrase are worth underlining and rereading over and over. They are equaled, if not exceeded, by his sharply drawn characters, who you will remember long after you finish this book."

—Bookreporter

"[*The Poison Flood*] had one of the most satisfying endings I've read in a while, capping what was overall one of the best novels I've ever read of modern-day rural America."

—Criminal Element

"In his narrator, Hollis Bragg, Jordan Farmer has created a compelling character whose personal story and damaged body become emblematic of a whole region devastated by environmental destruction. *The Poison Flood* is a timely and important novel."

—Ron Rash, PEN/Faulkner finalist and *New York Times* bestselling author of *Serena*

"*The Poison Flood* is thrilling, poignant, and full of music, a forceful counterpunch to the usual expectations about poverty, trauma, and physical difference."

—James A. McLaughlin, author of *Bearskin*

"Jordan Farmer's novel is both a gripping page-turner and a stunning meditation on body and place. *The Poison Flood* will punch you right in the throat with its honesty and its heart. Farmer is a singular talent, with a voice I won't soon forget."

—Nick White, author of *Sweet and Low*

"Once again, Jordan Farmer has written a darkly urgent book. *The Poison Flood* is not only a story about the redemptive power of art—it is itself a redeeming and beautiful work."

—Smith Henderson, author of *Fourth of July Creek*

"Jordan Farmer's immense talent shines with the creation of Hollis Bragg, an indelible character at the heart of this perfect ballad to rural West Virginia."

—Devin Murphy, author of *The Boat Runner* and *Tiny Americans*

"Once in a great while, a book appears that gives voice to multitudes living just beyond our everyday scope. *The Poison Flood* establishes Jordan Farmer as a writer whose lyricism and unflinching search for truth place him among those artists who carry our deepest concerns and very best possibilities across time. This is a profoundly good book."

—Jonis Agee, author of *The Bones of Paradise*

"A fascinating exploration of character, with a story that captivates with suspense and heart, *The Poison Flood* is a book about the influence of music, the power of art, and the complexities of luck. Irresistible and original."

—Timothy Schaffert, author of *The Swan Gondola*

HEAD FULL
OF LIES

OTHER TITLES BY JORDAN FARMER

Lighthouse Burning

The Poison Flood

The Pallbearer

HEAD FULL OF LIES

OF LIES

JORDAN FARMER

THOMAS & MERCER

Text copyright © 2024 by Jordan Farmer

Published by Thomas & Mercer, Seattle

www.apub.com

Amazon, the Amazon logo, and Thomas & Mercer are trademarks of Amazon.com, Inc., or its affiliates.

ISBN-13: 9781662509933 (paperback)
ISBN-13: 9781662509940 (digital)

Cover design by Zoe Norvell
Cover image: © CWP, LLC / Stocksy

Printed in the United States of America

For Paisley and Deacon

I

THE FLINCH

CHAPTER ONE

BOBBY WISE

If he ever needed a reminder of the infinite injustices present in the world, Robert Wise would recall that he was only seventeen and required a machine to breathe. True, he needed it only at night, but the ridiculous nature of strapping a mask on his face as he lay in the dark and listened to the hiss of oxygen pumping through the hose of the BiPAP was a heavy burden for a boy. Only seventeen and a machine keeping you alive as you slept. Just pathetic. A prime example of the world's unfairness.

More perplexing than the embarrassment of the mask was the cause. Bobby wasn't malformed in some way. A bit stunted compared to his father, who stood at a desirable six feet, and prone to the occasional eruption of zits across the bridge of his nose no matter how much he scrubbed and avoided greasy foods, but an otherwise normal young man. So when Bobby started nodding off in weird places, his father took him to a doctor who explained that Bobby's uvula was too large. The doctor held up his calloused thumb to model its size. Apparently when Bobby bedded down each night, his uvula partially blocked his airway. That left two options: an extraction surgery with a history of minimal results or the sleep mask.

No wonder Bobby's father took pity on the boy and bought him the bike. A secondhand hunter green ten-speed mountain bike Bobby had nearly begged for since he didn't want to be another loser waiting on the bus. The three-mile bike ride to school winded him, but it beat sitting on those vinyl seats inundated with the stink from generations of cigarettes. So the giant uvula led to the mask, and the mask led to the bike, and the bike eventually led Bobby to the witch.

Some might define this string of events as fate. Bobby might've even called it that had he the time to reflect, but pedaling his bike across town, trying to burn the humiliation out of his muscles, Bobby wasn't thinking about the possibilities waiting in his future. He was only contemplating what Ryan Wallace had said about the witch.

When Ryan came by their spot out on the edge of Copper Creek and told him a witch had moved into one of the old houses on Barnabas Avenue, Bobby imagined something spookier than Eliza Billings. Either the kind of gray-haired crone popularized by the black-and-white folk-horror films he streamed on Shudder or Morticia Addams in her tight lace-fringed funeral gowns. Ryan didn't have many details as he sat puffing on the cheap peasant weed he sold. West Virginia remained behind the times on marijuana legalization, and a town like Coopersville lacked the smuggling connections the college kids had up in Morgantown. Most local smoke came from an overheated crop of plants Ryan cultivated on the hillside. You could get buzzed if you smoked enough. Occasionally Ryan bought some hydroponic from the college kids, but he never shared this. The good shit was reserved for his own high.

That morning Bobby and Ryan passed a blunt of the peasant weed while Ryan pontificated about the witch.

"She's the real deal, man. Not just some black-lipstick goth girl. I'm talking an honest-to-God witch. Learned it from her dad, who was some kinda sorcerer or something. They sacrificed animals and hexed people."

Any news delivered by Ryan had to be taken with a healthy dose of skepticism. The boy was a notorious liar. Half the words that slipped through his rancid teeth were complete fabrications, and the rest were greatly exaggerated. Bobby hadn't known someone could look like a liar, but the word described Ryan perfectly. The boy personified mischief with his jean jacket, black heavy metal T-shirts, steel-toed work boots, and shaggy blond hair that gave off eighties-rock-refugee vibes. Ryan looked like the sort to stuff cherry bombs into frogs' mouths and set fires for fun. Keeping that reputation in mind, Bobby didn't get his hopes too high regarding the witch, but he did start riding his bike by her house daily.

Barnabas Avenue was in a state of renewal. Four years before, America had been hit by an economic upheaval the media took to calling "The Decline." The stock market bottomed out. Unemployment reached nearly 30 percent. Foreclosures spread like plague sores across the country, and with few other options, crime swelled. The catastrophe cleaned out the town of Coopersville, leaving few residents able to pay their mortgages or rent. Eventually the economy began a gradual recovery, and some semblance of life returned to the town, but the demographics of Coopersville changed from generations of mountain folks who were born in the valley to outsiders with considerable wealth. They poured out of the overcrowded cities, escaping ceaselessly rising rent, escalating heat, and devastating storms persisting from climate change. These new tenants snatched up the abandoned houses that had previously remained within the same families for generations. The outsiders changed the town, spending old money or lucrative paychecks supplied by remote work in finance, technology, or other consulting fees earned from businesses the coal miners, truck drivers, and machinists of Coopersville didn't fully comprehend.

Businesses grew. Schools improved. Almost all these changes were initially positive, but Bobby saw through the thin veneer of progress. The new grocer opening off the interstate was not the same as the convenience store owned by the family of Bobby's classmate Darren, who could always be found working the deli after school and stayed up late helping his father sweep before closing. That Black-owned small business, the sort of place the outsiders claimed to champion, was another casualty of The Decline. Bobby had a sneaking suspicion the new arrivals wouldn't have shopped there anyway. The newcomers needed beauty with their commerce. They required a selection of organic produce and in-shop baristas for lattes. The Decline provided them with the convenience of not having to put the drab local shops out of business themselves. They could lament the loss of small-town America while enjoying the benefits of cheap mortgages.

Barnabas Avenue was at the center of this change. The street was previously lined with turn-of-the-century coal company duplexes. New and more prosperous residents covered the crumbling block walls of the complexes with aluminum siding or tore them down altogether to build modern homes. The witch lived at the end of a small cul-de-sac in an impressive three-story house with a wraparound porch and two large bay windows that faced the street like watchful eyes. A moon-shaped portal sat neatly tucked just below the peaked roof. Bobby imagined the round window belonged to the witch's bedroom. Of course she'd be locked away in the attic like a deranged wife in Bobby's favorite Brontë novel. Bobby wondered what she looked like. Her father, an average man with a great paunch and a wispy blond mustache with matching ponytail, didn't resemble any warlock. The man wore billowing chinos tightened too high on his waist with a woven belt and often tucked in his striped polo shirts. Bobby had passed him twice in the local market and, despite the notoriety and rumor that preceded the man, found only another boring adult inspecting milk jugs for the latest expiration date. The witch was never with him. It took Bobby a week of riding by the house to spot the girl.

When he finally saw her, the witch was sunbathing out on the lawn in a white bikini with a pink cherry blossom print. She lay on her stomach, legs stretched out and tanning in the sun. Bobby nearly crashed his bike as he looked at the long arch of her back and the tiny mole on the edge of her left shoulder blade. The blonde hair she'd secured in a ponytail almost covered the wonderful imperfection. Bobby remembered the stories he'd read about medieval witch trials. Witchfinders said moles were another sort of nipple from which those who'd signed the devil's black book fed their familiars. Young girls accused of sorcery were carefully inspected for moles. Bobby understood this had simply been pretense for lascivious old men to glimpse covered flesh, but it was hard not to take the witch's mole as a sign. He realized he was staring when the witch rolled over and looked at him through the lenses of her red-framed sunglasses.

Bobby recounted all this later to Ryan as they sat by Copper Creek. Ryan skimmed the pages of an antique *Playboy* from a decade when the girls wore their hair in bouffant beehives. This seemed hilarious, considering Ryan could pull out a phone and stream any act of depravity he wished, but the boy claimed he enjoyed the magazines. "A glimpse into a time we missed," Ryan said.

"Chick has Grand Ole Opry hair," Ryan commented as he unfolded Miss March. "But I'd still fuck her. Look at those legs." When Ryan sneered like this, the boy reminded Bobby of one of the Sex Pistols, a band his dad liked. The Johnny Rotten teeth mingling with a moronic Sid Vicious grin. Still, the comment got Bobby thinking about the witch's legs as she lay sunbathing.

"I saw your witch," Bobby said.

"Oh yeah? Dancing naked in the moonlight with a black goat?"

"Lying on a beach blanket like Stacey Egan and the rest of the varsity cheerleaders."

Just the mere mention of Stacey Egan sent a perverted shudder through Ryan. Bobby didn't like Stacey. She was kind and sweet, but she'd come here with her father, who'd designed some sort of app and bought the old Hamilton house on Bradford Hill. Considering he didn't even know what happened to the Hamilton family after the eviction, Bobby resented her. It was unfair. Stacey hadn't asked to move across the country to some hillbilly shithole, but Bobby already understood fair to be a ridiculous concept. He didn't feel the same vehemence toward the witch, and that made him a hypocrite. There was nothing in the world worse than a hypocrite. Not a murderer or a liar or a thief.

"I think you've got the wrong idea about her," Bobby said. "Seems like a normal girl to me. Her old man is definitely normal. No warlock wears khakis."

"Looks can be deceiving. You look like a boy and not a eunuch. Why don't you talk to her? If she tells you to fuck off, then she's normal." Ryan licked a finger and turned the page to Miss March's turnoffs.

Most girls found boys like Bobby and Ryan invisible, yet the witch had stared at him from just above the frame of those firecracker-red shades sliding down her elegant nose, her eyes letting him know she saw him looking. It made him feel seen in a way he'd never felt with girls at school who always read the longing hidden in his glances. Bobby didn't mean to be so pathetic about it. He didn't stare or try to creep them out, but he sensed that he was simply too different, too much of an outcast to just talk to them. If there was a common response to his shy smiles, it was the pity of averted eyes.

The witch's look as he rode away had communicated something deeper, that despite his apparent desire to see beneath that cherry-blossomed bikini, she knew what he really wanted was access to secrets. The chance for conversation and acceptance. The look hadn't said *fuck off.* The look had been more of a question. *Are you brave enough?*

Years of insecurity had manifested itself inside Bobby as an internal monologue he described as The Flinch, a nickname the grade school bullies had employed whenever he cowered from their words or blows. The Flinch operated as his own malevolent Jiminy Cricket, a little devil perched on his shoulder that whispered doubt and despair into his ear. Whenever Bobby mustered the courage to try for a change, The Flinch reminded him of the futility of such an act. Whenever he felt a momentary peace or pride, The Flinch rose to undermine him. It was precisely The Flinch's influence that kept him away from Eliza. Each time he mounted his bike, The Flinch rode along as passenger, reciting doubts that kept him away from the witch house.

It took Bobby another week to work up the courage to speak to her. The next time he rode by, the witch was sitting on her front porch, her bare feet kicked up on the railing as she read a book. Bobby parked his bike at the end of the drive and stepped to the edge of the lawn. The yard was small, a tight square of freshly mowed grass that made his throat tickle. Most would've surrounded the miniature mansion with tall gates, but only a picket fence separated him from the girl.

"What are you reading?" he asked. Almost anything would've been a better introduction, but the girl didn't seem to mind. She marked her place with a finger and held up a thick paperback the size of a Bible.

"*Lonesome Dove,*" she said. Silence hung in the August air between them. She left the book aloft, waiting on him to continue the conversation.

"What's it about?" Bobby asked. Again, he felt stupid. He hadn't even introduced himself yet. Just stood on the edge of her lawn like an intruder. Bobby knew they had almost nothing in common outside of books. Ryan told him the girl devoured words as she lay sunbathing. Bobby made him note the authors and report back: Graham Greene, Albert Camus, Donna Tartt. Bobby remembered his experience reading *The Stranger* and how perplexing the novel had been until he read Camus's essay "The Myth of Sisyphus" and was introduced to the philosopher's thoughts on the inherent absurdity of existence. The dead author managed to say something Bobby had always felt yet failed to articulate. That aspect of literature, the ability to find someone who said the exact thing you always knew in your heart but could never muster the words to explain, was Bobby's favorite thing about books. Not only were you given another time and world, but you got to immerse yourself in the imagined consciousness of someone else. As much as Camus influenced him, Bobby preferred mysteries by Jordan Harper, George Pelecanos, and Walter Mosley, but books still felt like a bridge connecting him to the girl. Standing outside her gate, he was suddenly aware of his clothes. The fact that his jeans, holes in them out of wear and not style, were cheap and threadbare, costing almost nothing compared to the designer cutoffs she wore. Even her book was a crisp new edition, while the titles on his nightstand were hardbacks from the library, all wrapped in protective laminate and a week overdue.

"It's good cowboy stuff," the witch said. "But you don't care about my reading habits."

The accusation left him struggling for words. Bobby considered getting on his bike and just riding away. Only the girl was talking to him, looking at him with turquoise eyes that seemed able to read his mind. The corner of her mouth twitched up in an almost imperceptible smile that silently dared him.

"What do you mean?" he asked.

"I said, you aren't interested in my reading habits. Why not go ahead and ask your real question? Small talk's boring."

Bobby's tongue seized up on his words.

"Seems like it's a private question," the witch said. "Would you like to come up here on the porch?"

Bobby put the kickstand down on his bike. He walked across the grass with his hands shoved into the pockets of his jeans. Heat climbed the back of his neck. A trickle of sweat crossed his brow, and his T-shirt stuck against his damp chest. The witch looked cool and confident. She sat with the book on her lap, ankles crossed, as she waited on him to climb the porch steps. Even with plenty of chairs available, she didn't offer him a seat. Bobby tried acting nonchalant. He leaned against the porch rail and realized he was too close to her bare feet. He moved a few inches away.

"I'm Eliza Billings," the witch said.

"Bobby Wise."

"I know."

Bobby understood this was an important moment. He'd been granted an audience and had one chance. After that, he'd be back to riding by the house and gawking. The pressure didn't inspire confidence. Bobby told himself to fake it and managed to look back into those turquoise eyes. "I know you too," he said.

"You know of me. Not exactly the same thing. So do you have something important to ask me, Bobby, or are you really interested in my book? Maybe you'd like to discuss the decline of physical media? That's why I prefer the paperback. You can smell it, touch it, and put it on the shelf when you're finished. Or lend it to a friend."

"People say you're a witch." The words poured from his mouth so fast Bobby barely knew he'd spoken. He would've given anything to take them back. Here he was, in the presence of a beautiful girl, one who was really looking at him, really seeing him, and he'd blurted out the most asinine sort of bullshit he could've thought to say. Instead of having a real conversation, he'd debased her with town gossip. Bobby wanted to melt under the afternoon sun and leak through the cracks in the porch.

Eliza didn't look hurt. She looked bored, which was far worse. "Yes, my family is deeply into the occult. I've been studying various forms of magic since I was ten years old. Is that really your interest in me? How this can be anything other than slightly mundane in our current age is beyond me. I'd rather discuss books."

"That's cool," Bobby said. "I wasn't trying to be a dick about it or anything. We can just talk about something else."

"Oh, no, you were interested in witchcraft, so that's our topic. Do you believe in it, Bobby?"

Bobby didn't know how to respond to a question so loaded with implication. Eliza wasn't exactly hostile, but there was a playful nature in her desire to see his discomfort. He'd seen something similar in other girls who'd learned their power over him. The way some of them knew how badly he wanted to touch them and soaked up his sad adoration.

Bobby squirmed against the porch rail. "I guess anything is possible," he said. "I'm open-minded."

Eliza dog-eared the page in her book and set it aside. "I've got a page quota to fill, but why don't you come back later tonight? Say, nine o'clock?"

Bobby almost asked what they were going to do but managed to keep the thought in his mind and out of his mouth. Ryan had once told him that the terrible truth about women was there was nothing a man could do to make himself desired. More desirable, yes, but Ryan believed that women chose their men and that while you might make yourself a more appealing selection, nothing you could say or do could elevate you from non-option to consideration. The thought had struck Bobby with the deepest despair. What if he remained undesirable to all women? Ryan had only scoffed at the idea. "There's at least a few out there who wouldn't mind you, Bobby," he'd said. Bobby hadn't believed it at the time, but something in the way Eliza sat waiting on his response made him feel chosen.

"Nine o'clock. I'll be here. It's a date."

Eliza grinned again as if she found his attempt at boldness cute. "It's a demonstration. Don't be late."

———

Bobby rode out to Cooper Creek in a state of elation, legs pumping as if the bike could take flight and leave the broken asphalt underneath his bald tires behind. Ryan waited by the shallows with another *Playboy*. Watching him, Bobby wondered just how much money his friend's spank books might earn if he chose to sell them. They were rumpled and ripped nearly to pulp but might still be valuable. Bobby hopped off his bike without coming to a full stop and let it crash to the side. Ryan exposed the centerfold.

"Miss July. I call her Misty. Seems right for a redhead."

Bobby waved away the large breasts with sizable areolas Ryan hung in front of him.

"I talked to the witch," he said.

Ryan licked a finger and turned the page. Bobby had anticipated more of a reaction from his friend. Shock or at least pride that he'd gathered the resolve to speak with any girl, much less the witch. Instead, Ryan just perused his magazine.

"What'd she say?" he asked.

"She invited me up on the porch, and we talked about the book she was reading. I asked her if she was really a witch. I'm supposed to meet her tonight."

Ryan paused with another licked finger suspended above the page. "You said that to her?"

Bobby nodded. "I couldn't help it."

Ryan smiled that crooked, chipped-tooth smirk of his. "Jesus, son. That dick of yours must've grown three inches to suddenly be brave enough to do that. Aren't you worried about her old man?"

He'd been so excited to have the girl's attention that no extenuating factors, not even the father's reputation as some kind of necromancer, had bothered him. Besides, now he'd seen both the man and daughter up close and didn't understand what all the fuss was about. Surely all this witch talk was overblown. Eliza was an intimidating girl who no doubt trafficked in some peculiar hobbies, but it couldn't be much more than parlor tricks and little spells procured from the bowels of the internet. Magic wasn't real. The whole trend of young women taking up witchcraft was simply a model of female empowerment, the moniker of *witch* something young girls pulled on like armor. When it came to rebellion, the fishnets and corset tops were no different from a punk boy's leather jacket.

All this rationalizing sounded good, but it still didn't explain the contradictions present in Eliza. She hadn't gone in for the black lipstick and other accoutrements of the goth uniform. She'd worn the cherry blossom bikini like one of the cheerleaders. In the end it didn't matter. Bobby pushed his contemplation aside.

"I need something to impress her," Bobby said. "You have any more of that bud?"

"I might. How'd you plan to compensate me for it? I know you ain't got any money."

"Thought I'd rely on our friendship," Bobby said.

"Business is business," Ryan replied. "I can't just give it to you. I'd need some collateral."

"What did you have in mind?"

"I'd settle for a pair of witch panties."

"Be serious."

"Yeah, you'd never get that far anyway. How about your bike?"

Bobby looked over at the bike beached on the shore. It was his only means of transportation. He considered telling Ryan to go fuck himself but remembered Eliza's turquoise eyes as she sat with the book steepled on her knee.

"You let me hold the dope now, and I keep the bike till the end of the week. After that, it's yours."

"Deal," Ryan said, and produced a cellophane sandwich bag full of buds from his pocket. There was a sticky heat as the dank smell hit Bobby's nose, an overwhelming tang that made him feel lightheaded before he even touched the bag.

"You take care of my new wheels," Ryan said as Bobby straddled the bike.

"I might just smoke all your dope and dump the thing in the river before letting you have it."

Ryan only scoffed. "I'd follow you and that bitch right into Hell to get even."

Bobby knew it was true. His only real friend wasn't so much a friend but some sort of deranged juvenile delinquent who'd slice him up over a dime bag and ownership of a secondhand mountain bike. A better person would've just gifted him the weed, but Bobby didn't have anything better in his life. Ryan's circumstances were even worse. Maybe there was a lesson there about resilience or survival or just the predatory state of the world they lived in. All he knew was that he wanted more in his life. There was a time when he'd been so broken down he feared admitting that to himself, as if acknowledging the wish for a girl's affection and touch would somehow force him to face the reality that his needs were too far away, each desire something he couldn't hope to reach. After talking to Eliza, he'd felt a little of that burden recede. At least he was done pretending he didn't want anything substantial. He wanted the witch.

Bobby gave Ryan a final nod, then turned his bike around as his friend sat down on a rock and went back to his *Playboy*.

CHAPTER TWO

HARLAN WINTER

Right after my discharge from the psychiatric unit at Preston Hospital, I traveled down to Cheap Chuck's and bought my first pack of cowboy killers in months. The scarcity of cigarettes on the ward almost cured me of the habit, but newfound freedom made it seem like a good time to resume my more self-destructive impulses.

Cheap Chuck's was the last local grocer to survive the invasion of outside money. Like a guerrilla fighter refusing surrender, it remained the only place where a man could find a working Slush Puppie machine and buy scratch-off lottery tickets even as the boutiques and other artisanal peculiarities, places that would've been appalled by such appetites in their clientele, sprouted up around us. Chuck's been dead for a decade, but his daughter keeps a picture above the counter of the man shirtless on a fishing boat somewhere off the coast of Key West. He's smiling his gap-toothed smile underneath a broom of a mustache and holding what I believe to be a flounder. Next to this photo hangs the List of Shame. A scroll with the names of people banned from the premises for shoplifting, writing bad checks, or other misdeeds. They won't call the law on you at Chuck's. Just add your name to the list for public ridicule.

It felt odd being outside among people again. Even with most of the aisles empty, I wanted to retreat from the few shoppers eyeing beef jerky or refilling giant plastic cups at the soda fountain. I didn't speak at the counter, just pointed at the wall of cigarettes and tossed a few bills the hospital's intake station had returned alongside my other possessions.

The girl at the register observed me with the suspicion warranted a man recently released from the nuthouse. She glanced at the missing digits on my right hand, where the ring and pinkie fingers were absent. The cashier dropped the cigarettes on the counter alongside my change. The seal around the cellophane wrapper of the smokes said Nothing about Our New Packaging Indicates a Safer Cigarette. Using my wounded appendage, I lit one right in the store, thinking people should come with a similar warning.

———

Back in early January, I closed my bookstore and admitted myself to the hospital because I kept seeing the ghost of Brandon Flanders, a boy I beat nearly to death with a combination lock when I was just fourteen. The hauntings had started years before, during my experience with The Lighthouse cult. Back then the ghost appeared as a kind of harbinger, offering cryptic clues that helped solve the case of a missing artist and his girlfriend. Dr. McClain seemed to think this was an important detail. Why, the doctor asked, would a ghost who had little reason to be kind after the way I'd wounded him in life bother offering assistance with amateur detective work? Wasn't it more plausible that the phantom was some aspect of my subconscious working out the details of the mystery, and didn't the fact that the specter disappeared for so long after the case concluded prove this? Dr. McClain had some fine insights, but the man didn't make it easy conceding these points. The doctor was another transplant from the cities, the walls of his office covered in diplomas from Northwestern University, which might as well have been located on Mars for most of his patients. He seemed especially interested in my failed medical school days and time as a counterfeit country doctor. He treated the experiences as both noble and country fried, like something out of Faulkner.

There was less positivity about my occult studies. Dr. McClain thought it an unhealthy fascination, considering I'd been faced with unrelenting visions of Brandon's ghost for the past few months. I tried explaining how I'd been a rational man before encounters with the cult, and the ghost had created such upheaval in my life, but this endeavor proved useless. Dr. McClain didn't understand the way traumatic events could break core beliefs and mold you into a man you hardly recognized. Why would he understand? The doctor appeared insulated from calamity. Money, status, and the region where he grew up let him live without the kind of catastrophes people like me took for granted. Dr. McClain asked a lot of questions about class without explicitly asking. We talked about my other fights growing up and whether I'd ever hurt anyone else as badly as I damaged Brandon. For Dr. McClain, my history of schoolyard violence seemed a logical escalation to the act that left Brandon blind and bedridden. What the doctor didn't understand—what his coddled raising wouldn't *allow* him to understand—was that fights were simply part of life for weak boys like me.

Dr. McClain asked the wrong questions. He barely lingered over the abuses I suffered from my father. A mountain man living a life of criminality and regularly beating his son seemed commonplace enough for the doctor. Mostly we just talked about the ghost.

Brandon's visits, once infrequent, were now a near constant. No matter the hour, I could raise off the pillow and see the dead man hovering over the foot of my bed. Never a word passed between us. There was nothing left to say. I'd exhausted my apologies, and in the ghost's defense, he didn't really participate in any of the common methods of apparitions. No levitating household items or overturned furniture. No jump-scare crashes at midnight. Perhaps he was simply bored and needed something to occupy the endless hours of the afterlife. Why he came didn't matter. I found his presence intolerable.

Whenever we discussed the hauntings, Dr. McClain insisted on learning about all the minute details. He'd inquire about the smells in the room, the sounds as Brandon's ghost prowled the hallway with his nose bleeding that eternal flow I created when I hit him with the lock all those years ago. The doctor seemed especially interested in the fact that I saw the ghost as a man. The damage I'd administered was inflicted on a child. I'd never known Brandon as an adult in life.

"Isn't this more evidence of your guilt manifesting the occurrences?" Dr. McClain once asked. Cinnamon wafted from his mouth as he smacked his Big Red chewing gum and shifted in his chair. "Supposing the ghost is even real, a thing you've told us you never believed in before, why wouldn't this Brandon appear as the boy you knew? As the young boy you wronged?"

There was no logical response against this argument. I didn't believe Dr. McClain could help me with his pills and analysis, but I'd become so weary of the nightly visitations that I was willing to try anything. I'd decided that since nothing in my volumes of occult books contained the answer, I'd entrust myself to the hands of medicine I once so strongly believed in. If that didn't work, there was another solution. I could slit my wrists in Copper Creek. I'd already lost my fingers beside those waters. Why not let it take all my flesh?

The hauntings never ceased, but they did come with less frequency after treatment. Nightly visits subsided to once or twice a week. Hours of the ghost glaring at me in silence became flashes in my peripheral vision. I decided that was as good as it was going to get and checked myself out of the ward, thinking I could be equally haunted at home. Dr. McClain argued against this. He cited the fewer occurrences as proof the methods were working. I didn't bother to argue with him. You can't debate experts. Even if I was wrong, I was determined to return to my little bookshop and hovel of an apartment on the upper floor.

———

Life might have stalled forever if the warlock hadn't arrived. I passed three days in bed. Rose only to piss. Ate perhaps one real meal a day, if soup from a can counts. I took the pills prescribed and waited, but I hadn't yet received one of my visitations. Life continued in the same stasis I'd grown accustomed to until the morning I decided to go down-stairs and reopen the store. Thanks to my hospitalization-induced hiatus, I was totally broke and months behind on the rent.

Winter Books is located at the intersection of Wallace and Grand Avenue, the final block where the recent encroachment of progress had yet to take root. The bright shops catering to newcomers had not yet proliferated their sprawl on my side of town. I preferred it that way but knew it wouldn't last. Before I left for the hospital, change had surged over the old neighborhood, swallowing up our remaining institutions like an incoming ocean tide. I didn't mind seeing the once-empty shops revitalized. It was watching the old guard, the standards of our community shuttered and replaced months later, that pained me. McCardle's, a department store offering a whole block of shopping, including furniture, menswear, and women's fashion, finally closed and was replaced by a sort of upscale artists' collective where painters hocked prints and ironic T-shirts alongside a bistro and coffee stand. My father owned three suits, all purchased from McCardle's, and his bedroom suite, a gift for my mother, was acquired there on credit. He chipped away at this debt with slow minimal payments until he finally made a solid score robbing a jewelry store across the Kentucky line. Dad was smart enough to wait two months before paying off the remainder, but Mr. McCardle knew where the money came from and refused it, going so far as to risk insulting a dangerous man like my father. We never shopped there again, but I still hated seeing vultures picking over the remains of McCardle's legacy.

The only thing that kept my rent from climbing with the rest of the neighborhood was my relationship with the landlord, Mr. Isaac. I helped his daughter out when an old boyfriend kept harassing her, so he let me operate the store at a newly agreed-upon fixed cost. Mr. Isaac was already losing a lot by letting me stay, and even though I hadn't been evicted yet for being substantially behind, I felt an unspoken pressure to repay the debt. It was all precursor to the inevitable day when one of the out-of-towners would offer so much money for the building Mr. Isaac couldn't refuse. I wouldn't blame him when that happened. I didn't know how I would afford something else in town with the way inflation skyrocketed, but those were concerns of practicality. My rooms upstairs were just a place to flop. Mostly I didn't want the store closed or replaced by another outsider. I felt proud to be one of the last remaining local businesses.

My shop carried a musty odor that never dissipated regardless of my continual cleaning, but the front window was such a fine display for new releases it made up for the smell. Not that any of it mattered. I rarely had a customer. Coopersville's dedicated readers shopped online or at the Barnes & Noble near the interstate rather than browse my odd-ities. The shop specialized in occult works and books on magic—not the most lucrative topics in a small town. Any foot traffic was relegated to the curious hoping for a look at a local legend or shoplifting kids, brave little shits who risked having a spell placed upon them as they fled with whatever could be slipped inside a jacket. Expanding the stock beyond fringe offerings or maybe tearing out shelf space, inserting a few tables, and hiring a barista could've turned things around. But I didn't need grand success; I wanted only enough money to stay adrift. After my doctoring days ended, I needed to keep busy during the solitude. The empty shop sufficed. Nearly all my income consisted of online sales, anyway. Buyers found me through forums dedicated to paranormal research, occult message boards, and the occasional word of mouth that traveled the dark underground circuits frequented by wannabe sorcerers. It was a desperate little ecosystem that I'd somehow become part of due to my brief involvement with the now-infamous Lighthouse.

Dust thick as snow lined the shelves after my absence. A few books lay open, their crumpled pages spilling out on the wooden floor. That morning it was time to pull out my list of contacts and see if I could sell a few titles. As much as I despised cold-calling clients, I'd have to throw myself back in for cash.

When the door opened, I came around the counter, already apologizing for forgetting to hang the CLOSED sign. I draped the cleaning rag over my mutilated right hand. I'm still embarrassed by the sight of it and hide it whenever possible.

"I'm afraid we're closed," I said.

The man was stout and doughy, his tiny eyes hidden behind thick-framed rectangular glasses. He had a mustache and dressed in rumpled khakis and a blue denim shirt reminiscent of a middle school guidance counselor. A paisley tie too wide to be in style hung low past his belt, and a brittle ponytail, secured by a rubber band, draped down his back.

"Mr. Winter," the man said. "I'm Barney Billings. I'd like to speak with you."

"We should be open normal hours on Monday."

"I'm not here to shop," Billings said. He moved comfortably, stopping at the nearest shelf to stare at the leather-bound books. I remembered the revolver behind the counter. A snub-nosed .38 Special hidden in a hollowed-out book. I'd shot men before and wouldn't hesitate if Barney unholstered his own weapon and demanded the money from my register. Despite the wardrobe, I suspected Barney had plenty of money. Few have worse fashion sense than those too rich to consider the way they're perceived.

"Our coven just moved to the area, and I thought it prudent to come introduce myself to a fellow devotee of the arts."

I stifled a laugh. What sort of grown man, particularly one with the hair and attire of a youth pastor, used a word like *coven*? In my few years buying and selling books on magic, I'd never met anyone who referred to themselves that way. Still, I wondered how much he might know about me. My proximity to the events surrounding The Lighthouse was something I depended on for sales. Certain customers, those with a hard-on for true crime memorabilia and bragging rights garnered through owning a piece of sick history, purchased books from me easily acquired elsewhere. Only Billings didn't remind me of those tourists. Something about him felt too serious to be lumped in with the other gawkers. Like The Lighthouse's Pastor Logan, he was a believer. It explained our meeting. Seeking me out the way a gunslinger might pay an appraising visit to a neighboring shootist. Like the other occultists I'd met, I disliked him immediately.

"I just run the shop. I wouldn't call myself a practitioner of anything."

"Don't be modest, Mr. Winter," Billings said. "I know all about you."

When I didn't respond, Billings walked down the aisles, removing books from shelves, leafing through the pages, and placing them back without thought. He was clearly performing, a sort of reserved dance in his steps as he waited for some hint about how I felt being exposed. I gave him what he wanted and uncovered my mutilated right hand.

Billings tried not to stare at the missing digits, but I could feel his eyes crawl over my stumps.

"See," Billings said, gesturing toward my fingers. "That's true devotion. You lost part of yourself on the quest for knowledge."

"I'd prefer to have the fingers," I said, but missing appendages were the least of it. The Lighthouse's zealotry represented the logical conclusion for men like Billings. Each of magic's promised discoveries end in inevitable failure, but that doesn't matter. Hope fuels the internal fires until you chase the impossible like an alcoholic searching for the next drink.

Billings sat in the chair I kept near the counter.

"I wonder if I could persuade you to come by this evening? I think we share a common interest, and I'm sure the members of our circle would want to hear all about what you've learned after The Lighthouse."

There it was. The uniquely American fascination of sharing the room with the survivors of tragedies, making them relive the events of their trauma while the spectators siphon off the grief, circling like dogs waiting for scraps fallen from the table. All the details of Pastor Logan's crimes were well documented. The cult was obsessed with the idea of a spell that might transform artistic expression into reality. Paintings of crops that could make real fields flourish, songs about rain that could call moisture down from the cloudless sky, and dances that might raise those long dead from the grave. All that was needed was a sacrifice to accompany the piece of art. Those sacrifices were buried in a small mountain graveyard filled with Lighthouse pilgrims who didn't possess the artistic merit necessary to accomplish these works.

At least one decent book and several articles had been published on the events, but reading accounts wasn't enough for men like Billings. He needed to see the psychic scars I'd accumulated after entering Pastor Logan's basement torture chamber.

"We'd compensate you," Billings said. "One thousand dollars for two hours of your time. It's a small audience. Some dinner, a little wine, and conversation. You'd be our guest of honor."

I'd done plenty of things I wasn't proud of for money during times when I needed it even less, but I'd never debased myself in the way that Billings was asking. Sitting at a table among strangers, putting myself on display for the most painful moments of my life to be dissected. My pride couldn't permit that.

"I'm afraid I have to decline."

Billings nodded. He took a card from his slacks and placed it on the countertop. "If you change your mind, my number and address are here. Dinner starts at nine thirty. Come by anytime afterwards. We keep odd hours."

I didn't pick the card up until after he'd left. I busied myself with distractions, rearranging books and adding new stock alongside stock that would never sell. All artifice to keep myself from ruminating on the possible arrival of Brandon's ghost. Eventually I slid the card into my back pocket and went upstairs.

———

My personal library consisted of no more than eight books kept on a shelf in my closet. Not all the books had titles, but each a story. There was a handwritten diary of an eighteenth-century witchfinder that detailed his methods in locating and punishing those accused of witchcraft. There was a brief history on the customs of mountain magic that ranged from medicinal remedies all the way to spells that protected against evil spirits, wards to keep loved ones safe, and potions that promised to allow those who imbibed them brief glimpses of the future. Whether this future was absolute or only one possible future, the book didn't say. Another volume was the diary of a practitioner of dark magic who lived in New Orleans in the 1920s and eventually succumbed to vigilante justice. Of these rare texts, none were more precious to me than *The Conjurer's Guide to the Art of Creation*, the grimoire Pastor Logan followed and the catalyst for The Lighthouse's most horrible beliefs. I searched hard and paid precious amounts for the other books, but I suffered and killed to possess *The Conjurer's Guide*.

It was a pitiful-looking thing. The size of a modern paperback, wrapped in worn leather gone thin and soft as a vintage jacket. The pages yellowed from age and the handwritten text almost unreadable in certain passages. Just touch the cover, always warm as if the scarred leather made its own heat, and you imminently realized it was more than just a book.

I opened *The Conjurer's Guide* to a random page. Ran my remaining fingers over the cursive scrawl the unknown author penned who knows how long ago. As I began to read the words, I sensed another presence in the room with me. Brandon never arrived with a grand announcement. One moment I was alone; the next, the ghost stepped out from the corner of the room behind the small bookshelf. The apparition stood under the single overhead light, casting a sprawling shadow across the floor like a living man. He appeared wearing the white hospital gown he always wore. A stubbled, shabby beard covering his cheeks and double chin. The mustache of blood ran from his nostrils, the left nostril dribbling a little farther down until it touched the corner of his lip, reminding me of a clown's smile.

I hadn't seen the dead man in two weeks. It was the longest I'd gone without one of these hauntings, but something felt different. Brandon didn't simply glare at me. He didn't shuffle aimlessly up and down my hallway, traveling as far away as whatever invisible tether that connected us would allow. No, this reminded me of our first meeting, which had happened years ago in the basement of my father's house. That day, Brandon had shown me the lock with which I'd beaten him and forced me to remember the combination that would eventually free one of The Lighthouse's captives. Like that original meeting, Brandon had a message to convey.

The dead man pointed a finger at the book in my hand.

"The witch wants this book." The sound of atrophied vocal cords traveled across an incalculable distance until the words didn't seem to come from the ghost standing beside me so much as they simply descended into my brain.

The ghost placed his palm on the cover of the book as if swearing upon a Bible. A great despair filled me. I'd been popping antipsychotic meds for months and still the visions could drift in and out of my life at will. I placed the book back on the shelf and stepped out of the closet, turning my back on the ghost. It didn't matter. Brandon waited by the far wall next to the stairs, patient in the way only the dead can afford.

I took a deep breath and closed my eyes.

"You're nothing," I told him. "Whether a malfunction in my brain or some pile of ectoplasmic shit, you're nothing but old bones. Dead men can't boss."

I walked downstairs and sat behind the register, pondering on whether or not I could really leave $1,000 on the table. All I had to do was go be a spectacle for a bunch of magic freaks. I could let myself listen to absurd warnings from dead men, or I could get out of my own way and make some money. The real problem was my disdain for fellow occultists. Even if we shared an interest, I hated the things I saw among these men and women, their dogmatic belief in whatever supernatural fantasy that they wished would be true. The naked hunger for power easily gained by cheap spells or Faustian bargains. The truth was that before The Lighthouse shattered my life, I'd been a sane man who believed in hard fact. That was why I'd trusted the doctors to rid me of Brandon's ghost.

I tried reading some of my current novel but kept returning to prior pages, the passages lost in a haze as my attention waned. Something else gnawed at me. Billings had the audacity to come into my shop, but I couldn't find the bravery to expose myself for much-needed cash. Was it only pride, or was part of me still afraid to relive those days with The Lighthouse? Was I defending my privacy from opportunists or merely hiding in shame? Dr. McClain said that exposure worked as a psychic antiseptic, sterilizing mental wounds that would only fester without being addressed. Maybe the only way to truly exorcise something like Brandon was submitting the last of my rationality to Billings and his old gods of superstition? At this point, I'd pray at those altars if it offered a remedy.

A thousand dollars to have dinner and tell some ghost stories. Only a fool would turn the money down. I left the house, deciding I needed a bottle of wine to bring to dinner.

CHAPTER THREE

Bobby Wise

Bobby mounted his bike and rode toward Barnabas Avenue with the witch's invitation repeating in his mind like the refrain from a song. He'd decided to kill The Flinch. Cut it out the way a surgeon might extract a tumor. Whatever whole parts of him came with it would be something he'd accept. A final choice lay before him. Amputate his fear or let it metastasize into the death of his hope. There'd been so much waiting in his brief life. So many times he'd told himself "maybe one day" because a passive mantra and the hope for a better future felt easier than crafting worth out of the imperfect now. Coopersville was the cause of this. The kind of place submerged in regret. A ghost land where people waited on their remaining dreams to flicker out. The newcomers brought renewal with them, but Bobby wouldn't be allowed to drink from that well. That didn't matter. He didn't want a seat at their table. It was a place he could never belong, and even if he somehow gained admittance, he knew he'd be nothing more than a curiosity. What he wanted was escape. If he couldn't have that, there was at least the possibility of Eliza.

Prior experience had The Flinch whispering in his ear, telling him that the night would end in the same lonely disappointments of all the previous nights, but Bobby ignored that inner voice.

He made a vow to be done listening to doubt and stop flinching.

The witch was already waiting when he arrived at the house. She stood inside the gate with her hands hung over the wooden slats of the picket fence. Eliza wore an emerald-green cardigan over a strapless black top. A small bow adorned the cascading tendrils of her hair. She smiled at him, white teeth bright behind crimson lips. Bobby's Converses tiptoed against the asphalt of the street as he straddled his bike. The shoestrings were too long. The aglets chewed away by time, leaving the frayed ends stained a diseased brown. Even the prior bright-red canvas of the sneakers had faded to the copper hue of an old scab. Next to him, the girl was pristine.

"You're early," she said.

You've been waiting, Bobby thought. It seemed a cool line. The thing a more confident man might say to let her know he'd noticed the hidden gleam of her anticipation, but he kept silent. The Flinch called him a coward.

Eliza went down the fence line, retrieved her own bike, and walked it out to the street. The bike wasn't what Bobby expected. Eliza rode a hot-pink Schwinn with wide handlebars that held a wicker basket. No gears or hand brakes. The sort of bike popular generations ago. A girl of her station should've had a car. Maybe she couldn't take it without permission or wasn't trusted with the freedom of her own ride.

Eliza swung a leg over the seat. She still wore the cutoffs despite a chill in the night air, and Bobby couldn't keep his eyes off those toned legs. Eliza saw him looking, but she only smiled a little.

Don't get your hopes up, The Flinch whispered. *The witch isn't interested in you that way.*

But she was. Bobby could see it in the way she held his eyes. The attention she paid to the fledgling muscles of his forearms as he turned the bike. Maybe this was it. Perhaps he wouldn't have to keep enduring private disappointments.

"Where are we going?" he asked as they turned at the end of Barnabas Avenue and headed up the incline of Sage Street. Eliza pedaled hard up the steep hill. Bobby slowed, keeping her pace so they could ride side by side.

"You'll see," she said.

The quiet concerned him. Had he misinterpreted the initial comfortable silence for painful boredom? As they pedaled on, The Flinch whispered these doubts. It wouldn't go quiet, but Bobby let the intrusive thoughts pass through his consciousness without their barbed hooks securing all his attention. The pair crested the hill and let inertia pull them down the other side. Eliza's hair fanned out in a golden streak behind her.

As Bobby followed, the expansive lawns and high gates of the neighborhoods gave way to the streetlights of downtown. They turned down brick-paved Mason Street, where the first of the outsiders had opened their shops. Two delicatessens, a bakery, a coffeehouse with outdoor seating, and a boutique selling kitschy outfits for urban women suddenly finding themselves displaced in Appalachia and thinking it might be cute to play the stereotypes and wear a bit more flannel and denim alongside their leather. Bobby wondered how much the little prairie housedresses and jean skirts cost. He eyed the opossum mascot in the display window. As if any of these city people would know what to do if they found one feasting inside their trash can.

Did Eliza harbor some allegiance to the other newcomers? Yes, the outsiders were intruders, but they were still her people. Shouldn't that matter? Bobby didn't want to have to think about allegiances. He just wanted to be a boy on a date with a pretty girl. Only he wasn't sure that was allowed. Maybe it could be ignored for a while, but eventually reality would crack the fantasy.

"What used to be here?" Eliza asked.

"A pawnshop. Fred Childers owned it for over forty years. My father bought my mom's engagement ring here. Fred gave her a decent price when she sold it back after the divorce. Even sweetened the deal with a .40 caliber Smith & Wesson. Only gave her the pistol after making her promise not to use it on my old man."

"That bad?" Eliza asked. She wasn't scandalized by the story. Bobby wasn't sure why he'd told it. Eliza had been so forthcoming about her own upbringing that maybe he felt an obligation to hide none of his own redneck raising. It wouldn't have done any good. Eliza was the type of girl to see through lies.

"What happened to Mr. Childers?" she asked.

"Buried in the Memorial Gardens Cemetery for a decade now. I'm guessing his boy sold the place. You know the new owner?"

"We don't all talk," Eliza said. "Most see us as an embarrassment. Lots of ideas about tolerance until you have to invite the witches over for dinner."

Eliza rode her bike to the end of the street, stopped, and plucked something up from the curb. When she came back, she had a few stones in the wicker basket. She lifted one out, as smooth and round as something hewed from the earth could be without man's intervention, and offered the rock to Bobby.

"You want to be first?" she asked.

"What are you talking about?"

"Please. They come in, take over the local shop where your father spent his hard-earned money on a ring for the love of his life, and you're gonna let them sully something so sacred with a cartoon possum and a bunch of cottagecore bullshit. Now, are you gonna throw the first one or am I?"

Bobby looked at the rock in her hand. The way it sat comfortably in her tiny palm with the lacquered black nails brushing its contours. Just the chance to feel her skin was excuse enough to accept the stone. He looked up and down the street, searching for anyone passing by. Downtown received more foot traffic now than prior years, but the street remained remarkably empty.

A voice inside told him not to take the stone, but Bobby didn't recognize whether it was his conscience or The Flinch piping up to rob him of this chance at camaraderie through vandalism. In the end, he accepted the rock because he wanted something she'd offered.

The stone was lighter than he imagined. More like a hollow Wiffle Ball than a piece of sediment. Bobby rolled it around in his hand as he tried to muster some resolve. The street was empty, and the bike was fast. The stone probably wouldn't even break the window. Bobby closed his eyes and imagined the rock as it hit the panes guarding the beady eyes of that cartoon opossum that belittled his home and heritage. When he opened them, Eliza tossed her own stone.

The rock sailed in a high arch, lofting up until it nearly brushed the low-hanging power lines, and came crashing down just above the cartoon marsupial's right ear, where it left a hole the size of a fist. The shock of the blow reverberated through the shattered pane. Bobby watched the spiderweb fissures branch out like thin ice cracking until the window's integrity gave and the glass fell inward. Shards tinkled out into the street.

Eliza laughed and pedaled fast on her bike. Bobby almost tipped over trying to get his feet back on the pedals. Behind them, he heard movement on the street. Someone coming out to see what happened. He didn't look back, just pedaled faster as Eliza turned down an alley, putting as much distance between them and the crime as possible. They were at the end of the block when Bobby realized he was still gripping the rock. He dropped the stone as he followed Eliza around another corner.

Eliza stopped at the intersection of Wallace and Grand Avenue. They stood straddling their mounts, both huffing in an attempt to catch their breath. Wind-blown hair partially obscured the girl's wicked smile.

"What the fuck was that?" he asked.

"Exactly what you wanted," Eliza said. "I didn't want to throw that rock. I did it because you wouldn't do it yourself."

A perverse satisfaction that couldn't be dismissed as adrenaline had filled Bobby as they fled. None of the outsiders had minded pushing Bobby's kind out of their homes or businesses. The fact that Childers's pawn shop held no special allegiance or sentimentality in Bobby's heart seemed even more reason why the old man deserved to be avenged. Considering this, Bobby felt ashamed he hadn't thrown his own rock.

Bobby leaned the bike against a fire hydrant and sat on the curb. Eliza propped her bike on its kickstand and sat down beside him. Bobby smelled the sweat on the back of her neck. Noticed the dewy perspiration on her clavicle. He was about to say something, anything, to break the awkward silence when Eliza reached over and took his hand. The girl's fingers were cool and damp, as if she'd just washed them in a spring.

"Did I make you brave?" she asked.

"I'm not sure," Bobby said. It wasn't what he'd wanted to say. He wanted to tell her that he'd always been brave and regale her with some story of his courage, but Eliza was too smart for that. Those pale-turquoise eyes let him know that he'd have no secrets from her.

"Shall we find out if you're brave?" Eliza asked. When Bobby didn't respond, she leaned in just inches from his mouth, lips parted until he imagined feeling each of her exhalations seeping through his own closed lips. She held the pose for what felt like a century. When cowardice kept

Bobby from leaning into the kiss, Eliza pulled back. A disappointment so profound followed that the physical weight of it seemed to descend upon Bobby's chest. All those nights of teenage longing for just one chance at this exact moment. There was no gloating from The Flinch. No hissing in his ear about the pathetic, impotent nature of his failure. The defeat was so complete there was no need.

Eliza reached out and rubbed two fingers across his chin. Bobby didn't even enjoy the caress. He was too busy thinking about how his smooth cheek lacked any hint of stubble. Even at seventeen, his beard grew in soft and patchy.

"The man still needs some courage," Eliza said. "Let's make a deal. I'll give you another try. Would you like that?"

More than anything, he wanted to tell her, but Bobby couldn't find the words. Even his head felt fused at the neck and incapable of nodding.

"But . . . ," Eliza said, letting the word hang. "You have to earn the next try. There's something I want you to do first. A trial. A test of manhood." Her tone was almost mocking, as if she thought such tests ridiculous.

She stood and offered her hand. Bobby didn't look up at her, just reached out and allowed her to pull him to his feet.

"It's okay, Bobby. You're allowed a slow start."

He wanted to get back on his bike and ride home. Just sink back into the bored, celibate routine of Copper Creek and Ryan with his old-school jerk mags. Instead, he forced himself to meet her eyes. No look of cruelty or excitement on her face. Just a stern reverence.

"What's the test?"

Eliza led him across the street and around the side entrance of Winter Books. A single red door with a small four-paned window on the upper half greeted them. Eliza let go of his hand and removed another small rock from the pocket of her cutoffs.

"It's gotta be you, Bobby," Eliza said. "I know the guy is a local, and you probably feel some connection based on that, but I broke the window that belonged to one of mine. Fair is fair."

Bobby understood the need for mutual betrayals but didn't know if he could do it. Winter Books and its strange proprietor meant nothing to him. That wasn't the source of his reluctance. It was about what came after. Here they wouldn't simply be smashing some glass and fleeing. There were other things the witch wanted.

"You wanted to see some magic? That'll require supplies and a covenant."

Bobby thought about pressing his lips to Eliza's soft mouth. Thought about the touch of those cool fingers that handed him this second stone popping the buttons on his flannel shirt and examining his hairless chest. The Flinch was in his ear again, whispering all the reasons this was too much, too far to go for the brief chance of a girl's attention. In the end, Bobby didn't know if it was pride or lust or simply that vow he'd made to no longer be slave to The Flinch, but he busted the glass with the rock.

No alarms sounded. Still, Bobby fought to keep his legs from carrying him to the bike and riding for the safety of Copper Creek. Eliza, noticing this urge, put a steadying hand on his chest. After his heart slowed, she wrapped her hand in a bandanna taken from her back pocket, brushed the remaining glass from the pane, and reached inside to unlock the door. As it swung wide, Bobby crossed the threshold first.

The variety of scents inside Winter Books hit them instantaneously. Old leather and ancient ink. Wood polish and just a tang of spiced mint underneath the overpowering musk of pages. Bobby had always loved the smell of books. New editions carrying a warmth inside their fresh print or older brittle pages where the faintest hint of decay lingered. By the register, Bobby noticed a line of glass display cases containing charms and smaller pamphlets on specific magical arts. A tall display of candles stood like a tower against the far wall. Each had a tag below explaining the candle's promised properties and the proper invocation to speak as it burned. They advertised everything from true love to tremendous wealth. Bobby touched the wax stalks while Eliza examined the bookshelves.

So many elixirs, ointments, and balms all vowing to assuage nearly any human dilemma. In the end, Bobby supposed they were all the same dilemma. Men and women trying to duck inevitable pain. Watching the witch search the books, Bobby wondered if the girl really could offer salvation beyond his loneliness. Could she look into opaque crystal and offer advice on avoiding future pitfalls? Could she heal his obstructive airway? Maybe seal the spell with a kiss?

Eliza walked around the counter and took a large paper bag from under the register. She removed a hairpin from her cutoffs and worked on the glass case's lock. Bobby stood by, watching the practiced dexterity as she twisted and manipulated the pin. When the lock popped open, Eliza selected a handful of charms on thin silver chains, three tall black candles, and a few gems of which Bobby couldn't decipher their genealogy. Eliza dumped them in the bag. She went back to the bookshelves while Bobby stayed behind the counter.

"You didn't say we were taking anything," Bobby said.

"You're the one who asked me if I was a real witch," Eliza said. "And a witch needs materials. I'm going to show you something divine."

Guilt roiled in his stomach but not enough nausea for further protest. Bobby looked at the register. Likely, Mr. Winter had a safe somewhere on the premises. Probably full of cash stolen from The Lighthouse or simply pilfered away from the days when his father and uncle were working their highwayman routine and robbing half the county each weekend. Bobby's own father once told him that Abbott Winter had murdered a prominent criminal in Cleveland and returned home with a sack full of money in the back seat of his Impala, loot obtained either as payment for the hit or taken from the slayed man's own stash. Bobby wondered if the cash might be under the floorboards or hidden away in an old book. Some of the funds would've dwindled during The Decline, but some unknown income kept Winter's useless shop afloat.

Bobby opened books while Eliza poured dried herbs from several mason jars into a series of plastic bags. A few notes and other scraps of paper fell out of the books Bobby shook, but he stopped when he put his hand on a heavy leather volume under the counter. This book felt different, the weight consolidated at the center while the edges seemed too light. When he opened the cover, Bobby found the pages had been hollowed out. In the deep trench of paper lay a revolver and a handful of bullets. He touched the blue metal, rubbed a finger inside one of the cylinders, and felt the hollow-tipped head of a bullet. He was about to pick up the gun when Eliza spoke.

"No foxglove," she murmured to herself.

She wasn't looking at him, simply holding a mason jar aloft and shaking it so that the contents spilled around inside. Bobby stuffed the gun in the back of his jeans and dropped the ammunition into his pocket, where the bullets clacked together like coins. The feeling of the icy barrel against his warm skin was electric, the sort of tingling sensation only comparable to feeling Eliza's fingers graze his own when she'd offered him the rock.

"Come look at this," Eliza called out.

Between the rows against the far wall was a beaded curtain that led into a small hallway with a tight staircase. Mr. Winter kept an apartment over the store, but Bobby hadn't expected such easy access to the man's living quarters. Eliza was already through the beaded partition and climbing the stairs. Bobby waited at the foot of the landing, trying to think of some way to dissuade her without looking like a coward. He didn't want her to think his resolve was weakening now.

"Should we?" Bobby said. "I mean, we already have everything we need from the shop. Let's just go."

Eliza turned from her perch midway up the staircase. "All the real treasures are gonna be in his personal collection."

Bobby climbed the stairs, watching the muscles in Eliza's thighs as she ascended in front of him. The apartment was an open design with the living area, dining room, and kitchenette all connected. Only a small island separated the stove, refrigerator, and other appliances from a circular table with four chairs. The furniture advertised it as a bachelor's home. Few paintings on the walls, aside from a large canvas print of Dalí's *The Persistence of Memory* and *Spider of the Evening* Bobby recognized from a coffee table book he owned on surrealist art. Both hung unframed on the far wall above the blue sectional. Some bookshelves, but they mostly held paperbacks and a few nice Modern Library classics. Nothing that would quench Eliza's appetite.

They found what the witch was looking for in the bedroom closet. Bobby hadn't been paying attention. He stood looking at the partially unmade bed. The covers were pulled back on the left side closest to the nightstand, but the rest of the bed remained made, with the sheets tucked tightly under the mattress. This side was strewn with books and a few yellow pads of paper. One fountain pen, the cap left off, had stained the comforter. It was obvious no one shared Winter's bed, and Bobby felt as if he were staring into his own future—an empty bed covered in books and writing materials to distract him from the fact that he lay down each night alone. The only difference would be that his nightstand would have to make room for the BiPAP and mask. He contemplated this future until Eliza spoke up.

"Do you know what this is?" she asked.

Bobby turned and found her standing just behind him with a small leather journal in her hand.

"This book. Do you know it?"

"Looks like a diary to me."

"It belonged to Pastor Logan and The Lighthouse. Basically, it was their Bible."

"So it's full of stories?"

"It's a book of spells, but a book of spells specifically for artists. Some of it is open to interpretation, but the idea is that if you create a powerful enough work of art and fulfill the steps of the spell, it makes your artistic vision come true. Whatever you can render in art, this book promises to make it real. For a price."

When The Lighthouse disbanded, several bodies were found in unmarked graves behind the church. More deaths were rumored, along with a few other bizarre practices like locking the members of their congregation in wooden boxes for days without food or water in the hopes the pilgrims might have some revelatory vision. Such suffering confused Bobby. Weren't powers of conjuration supposed to bypass the hardships that accompanied real-life struggles? Magic promised a guaranteed outcome that real work left to chance, but it wasn't without its own sacrifices. Bobby understood that everything in life—even so-called magic, if it was even real—demanded some form of payment, and bodies in the woods seemed a far greater cost than possible failure. That was why the witch scared him a little as she caressed the leather book. Such reverence, for that was the proper word, shouldn't be taken lightly.

"We can't take that," Bobby said. "Winter will come looking for it. It's too dangerous."

Eliza looked disappointed. Bobby opened his mouth and sputtered some protest, but Eliza placed a soft finger against his chapped lips.

"I didn't come here for trinkets. I came because I knew that somewhere he had something special. This is it. Now, where was the bravery you had when I handed you that rock?"

Bobby looked over his shoulder at the half-made bed. The unfurled spot where Winter lay each night and the neatly tucked side where no partner joined him. He thought of The Flinch stopping him outside when Eliza leaned in to bestow his first kiss. Such a moment would be its own kind of magic, and as he'd already realized, all magic required sacrifices.

"Okay," Bobby said. "Let's check the medicine cabinet before we go."

CHAPTER FOUR

Harlan Winter

I'd been told all I needed to bring to dinner was myself, but I still stopped by Cheap Chuck's for a bottle of wine. I suppose I could've gone to one of the new boutiques offering more variety than Chuck's neglected bottles of merlot encased in dust, but I selected a decent vintage. Any satisfaction regarding the gift evaporated as I stood outside the witch's gate. I'd become strangely comfortable in isolation. All my recent conversations were restricted to group therapy or the occasional attempt at small talk in the day room with a fellow patient suffering from a Thorazine drool. I wasn't even sure my flannel shirt, dark jeans, and boots were acceptable dinner attire. Perhaps I should've worn a jacket or tie?

Barney Billings opened the front door with his arms wide in greeting. He wore a ridiculous polo tucked into his baggy trousers, this one composed of alternating thick horizontal lines of white and cerulean blue. His ponytail swayed as he came down the sidewalk to welcome me. Watching his khakis loft like boat sails with each step made me feel marginally better about not wearing that tie.

"I'm so glad you came," he said, wrapping his hairy arm around my shoulder and ushering me forward. "Everyone is going to be delighted to meet you."

The house was warm and inviting. The living room sparse with only two small suede couches and a leather reading chair positioned beside an antique coffee table. The walls were bare of pictures and painted in muted earth tones the color of clay. The reserved suburban aesthetic surprised me. The only garish flourish was a crimson Persian rug.

Barney led me into a low-lit dining room. Mozart played soft as a whisper from some unseen stereo, and two small candles burned on the buffet against the far, moss-colored wall. Three people sat at the dinner table—two women and another man. The women were both young and elegant in an understated way: the first, a brunette in a cream-colored blouse; the second, a blonde with large eyes, wearing a cranberry cashmere sweater. The man seemed at least two decades older than the women, freshly wrinkled and balding, aside from a little graying tuft that framed his ears and grew long toward the back of his neck. Their eyes followed us as Barney escorted me to my seat.

"Everyone," Barney said, "this is our dinner guest, Mr. Harlan Winter."

"Good evening," I managed, along with an awkward little nod. Barney pulled out my chair and I took my seat.

Introductions were made. The brunette was Olivia Homestead. The blonde Jessica Reynolds. The older man was her husband, Jeremiah. The couple had been part of Barney's coven for over ten years, first signing on when the group lived outside Saint Louis. Olivia had joined them five years ago when the family resided in a farm community outside of Omaha. They'd been all over, drifting in a sort of aimless way from one state to the next, concentrating on meeting others interested in magic. None of them ever stated it explicitly, but it seemed that The Lighthouse scandal had drawn their attention to Coopersville. I waited on questions about my encounter with the cult. Jessica seemed particularly enamored with my mutilation, those liquid dark eyes pouring over the missing digits no matter how often I tried concealing my hand under the table. We meandered through chitchat about the town's revitalization and my experience with those changes while Barney excused himself to fetch our entrées from the kitchen. He served everyone else before sitting. Baked chicken with garlic and rosemary, truffle-roasted potatoes, grilled asparagus, and garden salads.

The group continued to talk around me. Jeremiah held court for a time, blathering on about his early days as an aspiring alchemist.

"As absurd as it was, I miss it sometimes," Jeremiah said. "It was like living as a monk. Looking back, I think the outcome wasn't so important. It was just the dedication of saying 'This is what I'm going to accomplish with my life.'"

I understood the old man's meaning. My med school days contained a similar singular devotion until I'd met a woman, fallen in love, and let my studies atrophy when the relationship ended. Losing the ability to become a doctor hadn't been nearly as painful as losing the goal. The aimlessness of life has always been hardest for me, the idea that the only purpose we find is that which we assign. Perhaps that was why I found myself involved in this ridiculous world of belief. The appearance of Brandon's ghost during my days working as an amateur detective on The Lighthouse case made a profound impression and opened my eyes to the possibility of the supernatural, but there was always that resistance, the internal struggle in which the man of medicine pushed back against the intrusion of the fantastic. I didn't have the same desire for miracles the people orbiting my world carried. When I finally succumbed and opened the magic books, it wasn't out of temptation. The truth was, I didn't need to believe. I simply needed something to pursue even if it might be illusion. If my purpose wasn't going to be medicine or a woman, it might as well be the same miracles as these outcasts.

Soaking in their stories reminded me of why I hated these diatribes. Like The Lighthouse, they were another of the countless sects destined for misery because they couldn't fathom the unknown repercussions of achievement. What value would Jeremiah's discoveries bring if there was a known process transforming raw iron into gold? The problem with success is you lose the pursuit. With failure, you can plow on in vain. I could tell them about that from experience.

As Jeremiah concluded his story, the others provided asinine commentary about their own foolish experiments. Invocations and recitations for wealth or power, elixirs promising remedies to any health concern. All of this culminated with Olivia sharing the time she'd tried to conjure an incubus out of sexual frustration. I reminded myself of the money. When the conversation turned to me, I'd tell them all I'd seen regarding The Lighthouse. Let them have their fun. They'd paid for it.

I was enjoying my salad and ignoring their debate about some divination spell when I looked up and saw Brandon's ghost sitting in the empty chair beside Olivia. Blood dripped from his nose, speckling the back of his hands, which lay pale and flat on the white tablecloth. Those vacant eyes stared at me, pausing my fork on its way to my mouth.

"Mr. Winter," Olivia was saying. "Mr. Winter, are you all right?"

Brandon turned his head toward Olivia. I saw blood pooling inside the reservoir of his ear canal. Watching him leak, I felt the urge to lean over and dab his ear and upper lip with my napkin. That dead bastard never wiped the blood away. Just sat still as a portrait while each drop turned white hands crimson.

"Mr. Winter, you mustn't become so enamored with him that you can't join the conversation," Jeremiah said. "Poor Olivia has him positively spurting beside her and still manages to contribute."

My mind refused to process what the old man said, but I watched Olivia blush and place a flat palm to her chest.

"I don't mind," she said. "It's actually a little exciting. I mean, what a rare dinner opportunity."

The rest of them nodded along, acting as though we conversed about workdays or school assignments. Only Barney, looking across the table where Brandon occupied what should've been an empty chair, responded with the reticence the situation warranted. He watched my companion; eyes tracing over the slight movements of Brandon's head, following the long fall of each drip from his nose down to the bloom it spread across the tablecloth. How could they see? Months inside the hospital, pointing and shrieking at doctors, nurses, patients, anyone at all to notice Brandon, and I never received anything beyond a consoling hand on the shoulder or a sedative to relax me. Now, among these strangers, his presence was treated not as implausible, but a slight breach in dinner etiquette, the haunting a social embarrassment like not knowing which fork to use with my salad.

I considered all the angles of a possible con, but they hadn't tried to convince me of anything. The group simply reacted to what I'd already seen. Also, how would any of them know what I was seeing when I never offered any details? Jeremiah mentioned the drip and the proximity to Olivia without me saying anything about blood or seating arrangements. Maybe they could actually see him?

I pushed my salad bowl away and staggered off to find a bathroom.

I was at the sink, dousing my face with cold water, when someone rapped on the door.

"Mr. Winter, are you all right in there?" Barney called.

I swallowed a palmful from the spigot, sloshed another around my mouth, and spit. "I just need a moment," I said.

I felt Barney waiting outside the door, so I dabbed the water from my cheeks with the hand towel, ran damp fingers through my hair to fix the unruly tangle, and opened the bathroom door. Barney waited with his hands in his pockets, his eyes downcast in embarrassment at seeing me so shaken.

"You sure you're okay?" he asked.

"I think so," I said, but my voice faltered.

"Why don't you step into my study a moment?" That friendly hand was on my shoulder again, guiding me down the hall without me realizing I was being herded.

"What about the others?" I asked.

"They understand you need a moment."

The study was a cramped little room where bookshelves lined three of the four walls. Barney sat me down in a chair while he retrieved a decanter and glasses from an end table.

"Would you like a drink?" he asked.

"Please."

Barney poured us both a finger of whiskey. The Irish vintage warmed my throat on the way down but hit my belly hard, mingling with the fear until I sputtered and coughed like a kid taking his first sip. Barney patted my shoulder again and sat down across from me.

"You could all see him," I said.

"Yes," Barney said. "Who is he?"

I barely heard him. I was decades in the past, feeling the reverberations of the lock and hearing the sound of Brandon's skull cracking. There was a moment after that first blow when I might've stopped. Watching Brandon investigate his wound with trembling fingers, I could've begged his forgiveness, wrapped his bleeding head with my T-shirt, and helped him to the hospital. Instead, I only hit him again.

"His name is Brandon Flanders. He's a boy I wounded when we were kids. He's been haunting me since my time investigating The Lighthouse."

Barney took the chair across from me. He crossed his legs and rested the glass of whiskey precariously on his knee. "What do you think he wants?"

"I don't know."

"What do you want from him?"

In all my time in the hospital, the subject of Brandon was never discussed as a mutual interaction. We examined him only as a symptom that needed to be resolved. At best, the leftovers lingering from some deeper trauma.

"I don't care what he wants. I just want him gone."

"But why?" Barney asked. "If he does you no harm and asks nothing from you, why do you need him to go away? Aside from his presence, what's the concern?"

"He makes me feel guilty."

"The guilt would still be there."

I realized that I was embarrassed. I could deflect in the hospital, leave out fears or details. Tonight I'd been seen. Everyone at the party somehow saw my most vile act personified in Brandon's dripping nose.

"I want to show you something," Barney said. He took his phone from his pocket and pulled up a website. Pictured in the small screen, Barney and Jeremiah sat at a long desk with a pair of microphones in front of them. Both wore headsets as they interviewed another young man with sleeves of tattoos, his eyes hidden behind Ray-Ban sunglasses. Barney scrolled with his thumb, showing me an assortment of weekly videos with different guests. I recognized a few names. As I looked, Barney explained the podcast, discussing how each week was dedicated to a different practitioner of the paranormal or some witness of a supernatural event. He listed his favorite episodes, the ever-growing pool of subscribers and newest sponsors, but I was barely listening. I hated podcasts. Despised the endless online personas where authenticity was abandoned for outrageous caricatures that extended beyond the few hours of online presence into a permanent state of fraud. A constant performance that evaporated the individual for the sake of the brand. I came to dinner expecting my experiences to be exploited for entertainment, but I'd at least anticipated genuine interest. Now my haunting represented a business opportunity. The kind of exclusive episode that would drive viewer engagement and awaken the algorithms, but I didn't want to assuage the online vampires' craving for content.

"We don't have the subscribers I'd like," Barney continued. "But the fan base is always growing, and you're a name. Everyone knows about your experience with The Lighthouse. I think in the first episode, we'd just establish your story. By the third or fourth, we could be discussing the ghost and really building anticipation for the eventual ceremony where we exorcised the spirit. It could be big, Harlan. The biggest paranormal event in modern history."

His voice still carried the calm lilt of friendship, but I sensed a hardness in Barney's eyes. The mask was slipping, the goofy clothes and the congenial nature letting me know that behind this exterior lay a more calculating man. I would not receive assistance out of sheer benevolence. In a way, I appreciated the transparency. No more false camaraderie. I needed an exorcist, and he needed a freak to exploit.

I stood up from the chair. "Thank you for dinner," I said. "I think I'll be going."

Barney gripped my forearm. "Come on, Harlan. Don't be so quick to dismiss this. We can do a lot of good with a bad situation."

"You mean we can make a lot of money with a sideshow," I said. "I'm not interested in that."

"You misunderstand me. The goal is to get the message out there. If there's money to be made, it's only because we need more to keep things running. The sponsors don't pay for everything, and our coven isn't wealthy."

I pulled my arm free of his grasp. Barney raised a hand in apologetic surrender.

"Just come back to the table. Finish dinner and spend some time with us. Our world is lonely, Harlan. Don't abandon like-minded company just because I made a bad pitch."

Contrition may have filled his voice, but I'd become too suspicious to believe in any sincerity. My armor was on.

"Thank you for dinner," I said, and walked out of the study. I didn't stop in the dining room to apologize for my absence or make excuses for the exit. I detoured through the steamy kitchen smelling of fresh rosemary, cut through a parlor, and let myself out the front door. I was already halfway down the drive when I remembered that I hadn't asked for the money. In a way, I felt more entitled to compensation than ever before. What other guest could bring a ghost to dinner? Still, I didn't turn back.

CHAPTER FIVE

BOBBY WISE

They rode their bikes across town to the Memorial Gardens Cemetery. Eliza took the lead, weaving a zigzagging pattern across the road, pumping hard as the weight of the books and other stolen items crammed into the handlebar basket slowed her. Bobby tried to focus on the task of pedaling, but his mind kept going back to the burglary he'd committed moments ago. The night had not gone according to plan. All he'd wanted was some time with Eliza. Conversation and the chance to make her laugh with a joke. Feel the warmth of her hand or brush his fingertips along her thigh. All those unappreciated opportunities so often granted to the other boys. Instead, he was fleeing at least two felonies with a stolen revolver sagging the back of his pants. The short barrel poked the crack of his ass with each bump in the road. He'd known the girl was wild. The careless nature and confidence were half her appeal, only now he was indeed out of his element. Still, rather than making an excuse or simply turning the bike toward home, Bobby followed the bright curtain of Eliza's hair as it fanned in the wind.

The cemetery was located at the crest of a hill. One of the valley's few plateaus with adequate room for burying rows of bodies. The car gate was closed, but Eliza squeezed her bike between the tight gap without dismounting. Bobby did the same but scraped his leg against the cold steel, opening a small cut on his calf. They rode past the mortuary office and a pond, where a few benches had been set out for mourners to reflect beside the water. Ducks swam lazy circles across the placid surface in the day, but there was no sign of them at night. It made Bobby wonder where ducks went after dark. Did they roost in tree boughs like turkeys or bed down in dense shrubbery?

His grandfather was buried close to the pond. The man had survived three bullets during the siege of Bastogne and would've bled out in the snow had one of Patton's reinforcements not placed what he thought to be a corpse on the back of a Sherman tank, stowing the body away until it could be buried after the fighting concluded. Sometime during the skirmish, a medic noticed the ragged breathing and fashioned a field dressing. Bobby's grandfather woke weeks later aboard a hospital ship in the English Channel. He'd lost a kidney and lived the rest of his life with three scars like puckered mouths across his back. His grandfather survived all that carnage only to dig coal for a pittance, eventually choking to death from black lung—exacerbated emphysema. In the end, what was the difference in your blood melting the snowbank where you lay shot to pieces or drowning on coal dust in a pauper's bed? One could argue an entire lifetime existed between those moments. A wife, children, friends, and all the mundane enjoyment and trials of our existence, but Bobby had trouble entertaining that sentiment as he rode by the veterans' headstones, with their quaint crosses and tiny American flags.

After they had passed the modest gravestones, Bobby looked at the decadent memorials and mausoleums where the richer residents spent their eternity. Granite angels with spread wings and crosses that rose from the earth like some ruined ancient architecture. None of that glory did anything about the rot in the ground. In fact, Bobby found the grandeur a little pathetic. As if the inhabitants refused to mingle with common dust.

Eliza rested her bike against a nearby headstone. She removed the basket, collected a few items that were spilling over the sides, and turned back to see whether Bobby still followed. He parked his own bike next to hers. The drone from a chorus of crickets could be heard down by the pond, and a few fireflies winked their lighted organs on and off above the water. Eliza stood with the basket cocked on her hip.

"What now?" he asked.

"Now I'm going to show you what I promised."

After circling the pond, he followed her down the path to a row of mausoleums. The buildings were tall and thin, with a single great pillar on each side of the double doors. The doors themselves contained a stained-glass partition of tiny blue, gold, and red squares, but years of neglect had made the opaque glass too dingy to peer through. A chain and padlock were wrapped around the handle. Eliza took the pin she'd used in Winter Books from her pocket and worked on the lock.

"You're not serious," Bobby said.

The girl didn't look up, making it impossible for Bobby to see her face, but her shoulders sagged, and her voice came with the beleaguered frustration of someone speaking to an imbecile.

"It's time I showed you the things I promised," she said. "But if you're scared and want to go home, I'll understand."

Bobby dismissed the mockery and focused instead on the innuendo that might be present in the phrase "things I promised." Was she referring to some proof of her abilities as a witch, or did she mean the missed opportunity of their kiss? He imagined sitting on the dirt floor of that crypt together and feeling her lips against his own. The weight of her small, firm breasts in his palms. The slight moan as he pushed her back against the stone wall of the charnel house.

Head Full of Lies

The lock popped open, and Eliza uncoiled the chain. She let it hang absently from the door as she opened the crypt just enough for them to slide inside. She went first, turning sideways so that she disappeared by inches. Bobby followed without hesitation. The inside of the mausoleum was cold, and the air carried only the scent of old dust, not the decay he'd anticipated. The walls were tiled and the floor concrete. These tiles might have once been white, but years of neglect had left them the yellow of stained teeth. Two caskets, both a pale gray under the years of dust, sat in the center of the floor. Bobby had expected vaults or some shelf to cradle the bodies. He never considered the pair of coffins might simply lie on the floor forever.

But it wouldn't be forever, he thought. The crypt was well made and, despite their intrusion, preserved like any other sacred place, but time would take it. Eventually, the migration of men from one place to another would grind all these graves down into nothing. No one would cut the grass. No one would repair the eroded headstones. Weeds and animals would reclaim the land as they had the temples of antiquity. In the endlessness of time, not even the great necropolises remained.

Eliza sat cross-legged at the head of the coffins. She took two of the stolen books and placed them unopened on either side of her. Atop the left casket, she set a black candle and her Zippo lighter.

"This is the final resting place of Mr. and Mrs. McCabe. I did a bit of research about them, as it helps our ceremony. Mr. McCabe was born in Coopersville, but Mrs. McCabe came from Kansas. They met when Mr. McCabe was transferred there during his time in the army. They had three children. Mr. McCabe passed in 1985. Mrs. McCabe, a few years after in 1988."

Eliza removed a piece of white chalk from her pocket and scratched a few strange symbols on the concrete floor. She drew a small circle, placed another black candle in the center of the design, and picked up the Zippo. As she lit the candle atop the casket, the flame almost guttered out despite the absence of wind.

"We're going to call the McCabes forth," she said. "These earthly vessels won't rise. The spirit can't occupy bone, but with the right concentration and respect, we may be able to speak with them. In order to do that, we needed this book." She held up one of the stolen volumes.

For the first time that night, Bobby was more than a little embarrassed. What was he doing, sitting between two coffins with the weird girl? She still intrigued him, but he wondered how desperation for her attention had led him first to steal and now this foolish superstition that one could see as grave robbery. Eliza placed her hand just an inch above the candle flame.

"We, the living, beseech you. If you can hear us, please offer a sign."

It was the *beseech* that let Bobby know he'd been had. The word rang in his ears like a false note rising in the middle of a symphony. The girl was a fraud, and all this some kind of twisted joke that he didn't quite understand. Still, he went through the motions as Eliza reached out. She clasped his hand tight, her fingers warm from the candle flame, arms extended until the stretching strained Bobby's muscles. Eliza whispered something akin to Latin. Bobby wondered if it was more theatrics. Just some gibberish meant to help sell the ambiance. Outside, the wind whistled among the tombstones and slithered through the cracks in the mausoleum door. The chain swung in a lazy arc that made a mechanical, inarticulate music as it clanged against the steel door. Bobby opened his eyes. He made out a silhouette through the murk of the stained glass. The shape moved, fragmented and distorted behind the colored squares. Eliza still held his left hand, but his right reached for the revolver. Bobby pulled it from the back of his pants and aimed it at the figure. The shape didn't retreat.

"You broke contact," Eliza said with her eyes still closed. The door began to shake now as the weight of the figure pressed against it.

"They're here," Eliza said. "Come forth! We are ready to receive."

The door pushed open, and a figure filled the entryway. Impossible to distinguish much in the dim candlelight. Just a featureless face and hunched posture. The figure paused a moment, but it didn't seem to comprehend Bobby's unholstered gun. He still aimed the weapon, his hand trembling and his mind a stupefied blank. The sight before him dissolved all skepticism. The false promises of their stolen books felt like true prophecy now. For that hysterical instant, he believed the witch had called forth the dead. Obviously not the couple in the coffins, but her inexperienced necromancy had delivered this thing to the crypt.

The silence was severed by a scream. As Eliza wailed, the figure charged with its head down and arms stretched to seize the weapon. Bobby hadn't even known he'd fired until the sound of the pistol's report. It wasn't a conscious decision, more a reflex, a symptom of the forever-present Flinch. The blast inside the crypt was apocalyptic. Momentum carried the rushing figure two or three more staggering steps; then the body sprawled out atop the coffins, nearly knocking the lid off Mr. McCabe's casket. A dark confluence of blood and mud dotted the tile.

Bobby understood that he'd killed a man. There was no need to wait on Eliza's next scream as she huddled over the corpse. She took the dirty, stiff shoulders of the dark jacket in her hands and rolled the body over until she could see the face. Bobby wanted to look away but made himself bear witness. This was his doing. Whether out of childish fears of her campfire ghost story or some deeper propensity for violence he didn't want to acknowledge, the result remained the same. He'd killed whoever this was lying before them.

The dead boy was young, their age, and unfamiliar to Bobby. Probably another one of the outsiders Eliza had enlisted in her prank. A Coopersville kid like Ryan might've told Bobby about the plot out of some mountain code of loyalty Eliza couldn't risk, while this dead boy would certainly be ready to fool the pathetic country virgin.

None of this made Bobby feel any better about the neat round hole he'd put an inch over the boy's right eye or the gaping exit wound the size of a tangerine behind the opposite ear. Those were brains splattered against the tiled wall. Blood flecking against the stained glass. A great wave of nausea covered him until Bobby closed his eyes. The darkness didn't help. It only made him think of the permanent darkness in which he'd condemned the kid. Eliza had stopped screaming. Now she repeated the boy's name over and over. "Michael. Michael. Oh, Michael." As if this incessant repetition might be all she remembered how to say. After burying her head against the dirty shirt and crying, Eliza looked up. Bobby had always heard fury described as a kind of frenzy, but that was not what he saw in Eliza's eyes. The stare carried a resolve so strong that he was prepared when she leaped for the gun. Bobby was small, but enough fights with bullies had left him aware of the necessity for sucker punches and low blows. He bashed Eliza in the nose with the butt of the revolver. She fell back against the tiled wall, the drip from her nose painting her bare thigh.

"I need you to be calm," Bobby said. There was little authority in his voice. Had he been her, Bobby would've simply wiped the blood away and made another try for the pistol. The body was probably the only thing that stopped her.

"I only wanted to scare you," Eliza said.

Bobby didn't point the gun but let the barrel sway in her general direction as a deterrent from further outbursts.

"Scare me how?"

Eliza refused to answer.

"Scare me how?" Bobby asked again.

"Lock you inside."

The cruelty of it surprised him. He didn't know how to respond. There was only the feeling of his trust leaving, something regressive and permanent like a diamond diminishing back to its prior state of coal. A night inside a crypt with two corpses and only two candles guaranteed to extinguish as the hours bore on.

"You really would've done that to me?"

"I needed the books."

He'd wanted to imagine some element of her performance was a real spark of interest, but would she have even shed a tear if this boy had wrestled the gun from him and shot Bobby down? Not likely. The Flinch whispered with a new conviction now. It told him he might as well put the warm barrel in his own mouth. He was a murderer, and she was a witness. But Bobby was too cowardly for that. Instead, he slid the revolver into the front of his pants.

"I'm going to move him behind one of these coffins," he said, nodding at the dead boy. "You're going to help me. After that, I want to know what's really so important about those books."

CHAPTER SIX

Eliza Billings

From her earliest years, Eliza knew her family was different. It wasn't just the cycle of nonrelations who lived with them in their series of rented homes, each individual coming and going with no more concern than a nomadic whim. It was the way the other kids watched her. Eliza only ever saw them from a distance. The coven's isolation left her shielded from the outside world's normalcy. No school but her inadequate homeschooling. All outside trips quick runs through the department store or grocer's, stocking up on the essentials. The coven never socialized with anyone aside from other seekers and easy marks whom they could convert or at least fleece for a little money with promises of fortune-telling, metaphysical charms, and potions guaranteed to provide nearly anything the heart desired.

All this could be weathered, but it was the hypocrisy that left a sour taste in Eliza's mouth. Her days operated in a lazy routine of lies. Homeschooling assignments passed the daylight hours, and early bedtimes reigned until she reached ten years old and her father began letting her study the tamer rituals. Nothing too provocative for her initiation. Things changed slowly. Eliza finally sat at the adults' table during dinner party debates. She also received a few books on the history and essential properties of magic. After working her way from Crowley through the rest of the modern era, she attended a series of séances and spells that achieved nothing substantial.

This lifestyle had its romantic charms, but doubt festered within Eliza. Her parents couldn't hide her from the unrelenting influence of the mundane world. She wasn't forbidden things. Not forced into an antiquated lifestyle like some religious sects that shun modernity. She was simply too weird for companionship. What did cool clothes matter if she lacked girlfriends to compliment her outfits? Why bother learning the songs on the radio with no one else to sing along or go to the movies without a partner sitting next to you in the dark?

Even though they never spent more than a few months in each town, Eliza heard the whispers. Rumors swirled until the coven packed up and moved on. As she grew, it occurred to Eliza the coven must be running from something. Why all the dilapidated hick towns, the Rust Belt hovels with the remnants of their dead industries, or the country backwoods, where their practices seemed so alien? Why not disappear into a city where anyone could find some acceptance and assimilate no matter how bizarre their beliefs? Surely a metropolis would provide sanctuary. But the coven never settled down in populations over a hundred thousand people, as if a defined skyline signaled present danger.

Sometimes members stayed behind or left the lifestyle completely. Eliza envied that freedom. She wanted the experiences other girls received. If only the endless travel would stop long enough for her to make a friend. None of the current members of the coven had children. There'd been one other girl when she was little, a tiny redhead named Charlotte who rarely spoke and refused to play with her no matter how much Eliza tried being friendly. She offered Charlotte her toys, acquiesced to any games the girl might approve of, and asked questions despite Charlotte's stern silence. Anything and everything she thought might please the girl was attempted, and still Charlotte never warmed to her. Charlotte and her mother left them in Kansas to go back to Louisiana, and it was the last Eliza ever saw of the girl.

The next closest thing she'd had to a friend was a half-dead chestnut tree sagging over the roof of the house they'd rented in Georgia. The tree was afflicted with some unknown disease that left it mostly leafless and barren until it dropped nuts and sharp spiked burrs onto the ground in October. On more than one occasion, Eliza's mother removed these burrs from her foot with tweezers, but Eliza didn't care. She'd grown so lonely by that point even an offering of pain felt like a precious gift. When they'd left the house, Eliza wept, realizing she'd never climb into the bough of that old tree again.

She played the part of devoted daughter, but all these desires were locked away inside. It helped that her mother was in charge of her instruction. Unlike the rest of the coven, her mother made an attempt with neighbors. She attended book clubs or baking classes despite her husband's disapproval of her absence from home, but these hopes for some acceptance never worked. Most scorned her completely regardless of the town, and the few friends she did make always seemed to lose interest or were forgotten when the coven relocated. It was no real surprise to Eliza when her mother departed after Nebraska. There were promises to visit. A few FaceTime calls in the early days, but within a year the weekly talks had dwindled down to monthly obligations. After a few more months, all links were severed. Eliza wouldn't know for another two years, but her mother had met a man. Not a practitioner like her father. An attorney with a son from a prior marriage. Eliza longed to be part of this new family. A boring stepfather and a stepbrother sounded like exactly what she wanted. Naturally, she blamed her father. He was the true believer. He was the one who wouldn't let the family develop roots or integrate into society. He kept her homeschooled and drifting from place to place before any friendships could be established. So when the family settled in Coopersville, she'd leveraged all this angst against him until her father relented and let her go to public school.

She had a few months before summer school began—something she was excited to enroll in—so Eliza made a study of popularity. Rather than strange outsider, she'd become something loved and envied. Eliza scoured the internet for advice. The rabbit hole was deep. Endless content of all types regarding any imaginable topic, all by girls who seemed to suffer from the same social stigmas. None believed in their beauty or intelligence or worth. Naked vulnerability or cringe-inducing arrogance were the norm. Eliza resisted this. She didn't want weakness yet hoped to develop the girls' false confidence. She watched countless TikTok videos of other teenagers and mimicked their interests, mannerisms, and style. Something about the performative nature of it sickened her. The girls seemed more hashtag than person, but there were also startling moments of truth. Not in the bullshit they spewed, but in the humanity that couldn't be hidden under the layers of fabricated prestige.

Before they reached Coopersville, she'd constructed an entire algorithmically influenced persona. A kind of flesh avatar that would keep the others from seeing the true shy girl underneath. The problem was that her reputation preceded her. All the other kids in town already knew about her background. Most had streamed episodes of her father's podcast within a week.

The podcast was a serious point of contention in the coven. Multiple members had abandoned them after her father made the first few episodes, which were dull and contained an uneven aesthetic where her father transitioned between sounding like a cult leader speaking prophecy to those in his thrall and a professor lecturing on the history of mysticism. It wasn't until the third month of weekly episodes that her father decided to host other occultists. Things grew more polished. Her father descended into fewer tangents and brought on more guests. His followers slowly increased. While he gained subscribers, Eliza continued to be either an object of only mild interest or apathy for the other misfits at summer school. No one cared about a teenaged witch. They were already transfixed by their phones' ability to conjure.

The only person who took an interest in her was Michael Hartman. He'd cornered her in the stairwell just after biology, standing at the second flight of steps and blocking her ascent with wide arms that bridged the handrails. The boy's oversize teeth and slightly pointed canines left his grin sharklike. A scruff of adolescent beard speckled his face. It simultaneously repelled and attracted Eliza. A promise of the full beard he might grow in a few years' time.

"Move, fucker," she'd said.

Michael only smiled. "You don't hang with anybody, do you?"

Eliza stood with her books clasped across her chest as Michael stared down her blouse.

"No friends or boyfriend. Guess you have to get off riding your broom."

"Better than your dick," she said. If she'd learned anything from the TikTok videos, it was never to show the bullies weakness. Michael moved aside, and she passed by, reminding herself not to look back. Still, she could feel eyes on her the whole way down the hall toward calculus.

Michael made his next attempt later that week. He'd revised his tactics, coming upon her as she sat on the lawn of Coopersville High, making notes in her copy of *Macbeth*. She felt absurd when he saw her reading it, particularly since the Weird Sisters were reciting one of their many prophecies.

"About the other day," Michael said as he looked around the lawn to see if they were being watched. "I just wanted to get your attention. I think you're cool."

Michael was not cool. He was tall and strangely handsome but in an insecure and imprecise way. Girls would've liked him had he carried himself with a little more confidence. In fact, Eliza decided she preferred the rudeness of their previous encounter. Here on the lawn, hands hidden in his jean pockets, shoulders shrugged as he looked down on her, Michael lost any sense of authority. He looked like the boy he was.

"I'm not cool," Eliza said. "I'm the weird witch girl of Coopersville High. Sounds like a bad teen drama."

Michael chuckled, maybe a little too hard for the poor joke, she thought. The smile made him beautiful for just an instant. Neither an awkward teenager nor cocky hallway antagonist. For a moment, he was all dimples and teeth.

"Can I sit?" he asked.

Eliza patted the crabgrass beside her. Michael didn't sit close, but she felt the electricity in the air at his proximity, the hormonal maelstrom as they sat silent—her reading the book and Michael appearing deep in his thoughts, probably considering the right thing to say, perhaps working up the courage to slide close and place a hand on her bare knee. This must be the thing the girls online went on about. This pain in her stomach and stirring she felt at the smell of him, that distinctly male odor just underneath the clean soap and acne cleanser. Nothing more happened that day, but he was constantly in her thoughts the next few weeks.

Any spare evening moment was spent with him. Michael was too poor to own a car, but Eliza biked over each afternoon. They met at the end of his street. The pair never went to Michael's house. Eliza never met his parents, and taking him home to the coven was unthinkable. Michael never asked. Never mentioned the coven at all after that initial moment in the stairwell. The only other time he referenced her identity as a witch was the time they had sex.

The event was unplanned. They'd been out in the woods, engaged in their usual routine of kisses and dry humping, when desire surpassed better judgment. The whole thing was fast and unskilled, the sort of fumbling and lurching act that ended with them lying in the weeds in a state of confusion. Eliza felt most girls would've wanted something more ideal for a first time, but she felt content lying beside him as they pulled their clothes back into place. There had been pain, but she'd become aware of the pleasure just underneath this pain. The next time would be better. Not so rushed and awkward. Knowing this somehow reduced any disappointment. Everything would've been fine if Michael hadn't spoken.

"It's true about you," Michael said. "I'm bewitched."

The comment was meant as a corny endearment but raised instant revulsion inside Eliza. She left without explanation and avoided him for four days, refusing to return texts or speak to him until he ambushed her in the school stairwell again.

"The fuck is your problem, bitch?" he asked.

Eliza had expected this. Such an immature reaction was, if not to be understood, at least anticipated from a boy unsure why this girl who'd wanted him so badly days ago in the woods no longer looked at him with the same raw hunger. If Eliza understood better herself, she might've given him an explanation. She brushed past him, secure in the certainty he'd let her despite the insult. When Eliza turned back, he was looking after her with full eyes, his Adam's apple bobbing as he tried swallowing the coming tears down a hot throat.

"Why won't you text back?" he asked.

She was late the next week. Her cycle was always consistent. A night of cramps accompanied by small blotches that stained the inside of her panties and a heavier, middle-of-the-night flow that always woke her.

When she got up the next morning without blood, she knew. Some girls said that you could tell only days later. Not the stomach cramps, tender breasts, and fatigue, but a fullness inside that let you know you were no longer just yourself. Eliza didn't feel anything like that. If she thought of anything, it was parasites. Those worms that burrow into the brains of other insects and manipulate their flesh until the ant or snail is nothing more than a necrotic puppet. In a way, she understood that something significant like this pregnancy had been necessary. People will sit in their cages and find ways to tell themselves that the lost freedom isn't that bad. Twice as easy for those born into these shackles. It takes something like this to make a person decide they have to take drastic, perhaps even revolutionary, action. She didn't want a baby, but most of all, she didn't want another child to grow up in the coven. Her father held no pro-life opinions. No moral stance against abortion or anything else particularly. If Eliza had to classify her father's politics, the closest thing to any school of thought would be anarchy. A "do as you will" kind of belief. But another member of the coven, particularly a blood relation who would never leave him, was too precious to lose. He'd make her keep it.

Eliza plotted the whole way to the pharmacy. She needed money. The coven had little savings left after purchasing the house. Ironic that the roots her father promised finally came at so inopportune a time. She might be able to steal enough pocket change to flee, but not for the procedure and any kind of sustained existence afterward. For that, she'd need real money.

Inspiration came to her on the ride back with two pregnancy tests tucked into the pocket of her jeans. The closest state with abortion access was Pennsylvania, but for money she was thinking of Mr. Clark in Florida. Mr. Clark was one of the many occultists scattered across America whom her father knew. They had traded rare books on occasions, but their relationship ended when it became more one of rivalry than friendship. Eliza didn't know why, but an unspoken animosity had accompanied all their dealings. It went beyond good-natured competition. Sometimes she thought Mr. Clark might wish misfortune on her father. What he wouldn't do was return a lost daughter. Especially if she came bearing an irresistible gift. Mr. Clark had an extensive book collection. A massive private library with early editions of the canonical magical works, a few handwritten French manuscripts from a group of warlocks who died together when they accidentally burned down a Parisian hotel, and a series of written confessions from young colonial women tried as witches. These were the pride of the collection. Apparently, the witches had included many of their spells in order to give the witchfinders more knowledge on the powers they gained after signing the devil's book. Mr. Clark had been methodically trying the spells for years, attempting to weed out the coerced lies from the real magic. If she brought an offering, he might give her sanctuary just out of spite, but nothing in the coven's library would be adequate.

At home, she pissed on the two test strips and waited. Eliza let herself cry a little when the matching pink line from the first test appeared on the second, but only briefly. Tears wouldn't solve anything. She needed to think of something worthy for Mr. Clark.

Three days later, her father told Mr. Reynolds that he planned to invite Harlan Winter to dinner in the hopes the man might appear as a guest on the podcast. Eliza had heard the rumors about the man who ran Winter Books. She knew that he'd nearly been a doctor and that years ago he'd been involved in the murders surrounding The Lighthouse cult. Mr. Clark had the same preoccupation with The Lighthouse as everyone in her father's circle. So when her father said he planned on inviting Mr. Winter to dinner at the end of the week, Eliza knew that was her opportunity. With the right book for Winter's collection, particularly something related to The Lighthouse, Mr. Clark would pay a heavy premium, and she'd have money for wherever she wanted to go next.

The problem was knowing the coven would keep looking. What she really needed was to disappear. Evaporate like steam until there was no trace of her. There were spells in her father's books that claimed to offer such abilities, but she'd seen enough to know magic held only empty promises. The world was what we made it. Our potential often nothing more than what we failed to achieve. Money and grit would be her salvation. Not charms or incantations.

The plan came to her when Eliza noticed Bobby Wise riding by on his bike. The pregnancy left her feeling awkward about sunbathing. Even without her body showing any signs of change, there was a fear of being bare in front of anyone. Eliza scrutinized herself in the bathroom's full-length mirror every time she changed into the bikini. The little things she'd always hated were still present. The loosening skin on the underside of her arms, for which the TikTok girls had promised several remedies. The tiny dab of fat at the very top of her thighs that felt independent of muscles and would never leave no matter how much she exercised. What she didn't see was any bloat in her belly. It remained hard and flat, not yet swelling with the growing child.

The first time Bobby rode by, Eliza pretended not to notice his slow pedaling. She kept reading *Lonesome Dove*, a strange affection growing toward Lorena. Another woman in an impossible situation with limited options. She stayed buried in the book as Bobby cruised by. Eliza arched her back and stretched out her legs, letting the boy watch. His gaze carried more charge than Michael's touch, and his need felt so desperate it made Eliza more than a little embarrassed. She hoped to never feel anything so intense as his longing. Still, it was flattering. Bobby wouldn't be disgusted with the little bits of fat on her thighs. He'd beg to place them in his mouth.

Eliza knew she'd found her mark. Convince Bobby to break into the bookstore, subdue him later in the graveyard, and let him wake surrounded by items from Winter's and the bloody rags of her clothing scattered across the tombstones. The police wouldn't look further. Bobby would swear he didn't know what happened, but who'd believe him? He'd be just another inmate who never revealed where the bodies were buried. Perhaps she'd leave something irrefutable behind. Would she really miss a finger?

Ideas were coalescing until the day Michael came upon her sunning. She wore her cutoffs and bikini top again with *Lonesome Dove* resting beside her. Michael hopped the fence.

"Why won't you even talk to me?" he asked as his long shadow stretched across the blanket. "What did I ever do to you?"

She wanted to tell him he'd infected her with his juvenile bastard and ruined what life she'd managed to salvage, but she felt a sudden empathy toward him. He'd been stuck in similar drab circumstances, trapped in a hick town with nothing to look forward to but varsity football and a cheerleader turned ex-wife who'd provide ungrateful sons and defiant daughters. Another generation angry that the last couldn't save them from a poor birthright. Michael had built her into something exotic. A literal witch from a fable settled down in his little Podunk backyard. All this made it hard to yell at him, but he'd scare Bobby off if the boy came by again. Michael was no substitute for Bobby. She might be able to manipulate this stronger boy into robbery with promises of love and sex, but she needed Bobby if she wanted a fall guy the town wouldn't question.

"You didn't do anything to me," she told him. "You just need to realize I'm not worth it. You're doing all this pointless pining, embarrassing yourself because one fucked-up girl won't call you back. You're a good-looking guy. You can still get laid. It's not a big deal."

Michael opened his mouth for some debate, but she cut it down. "I don't have time for this," Eliza said.

A brief moment passed where she thought he might hit her. It was the next step up from cruel words and stalking, but Michael only stood staring down at her exposed body with a kind of bewildered silence.

If Eliza had been a little wiser, she'd would've known that wasn't the end. Michael's absence the next few days made it easier to disregard their fight, but she'd felt his presence all evening. Leaving Winter's, Eliza thought she saw Michael lurking on the street. She dismissed this as paranoia. The boy wasn't watching her. No one knew about her plans in the cemetery. Still, Eliza hadn't been completely surprised when Michael came into the crypt. Whether tailing her from earlier that evening when she'd left her getaway bag among the tombstones or following from Winter's didn't really matter. She could've handled the boy's jealousy. She just hadn't anticipated the pistol.

When Bobby aimed the gun, Eliza only watched with morbid fascination. She wasn't shocked when it happened. Fear can prompt even the weakest of us to self-defense, but the change afterward, the way he'd bashed her nose and sat with the gun absently trained on her, felt like a complete metamorphosis.

They pulled Michael's body behind the caskets and sat back down, careful to avoid the bloodstains. Bobby's hand grasping the revolver trembled slightly, but Eliza suspected that was adrenaline and anger rather than fear.

"What did you two have planned?" Bobby asked. "Lock me in here and get a good laugh? Maybe snap some photos for all your friends?"

Was the boy such a victim he couldn't imagine being exploited for anything more than sport? She wanted to alleviate him of this idea. Let him know not everyone who manipulates does so out of cruelty. It hadn't been personal. She didn't deride him for his weakness. She'd needed to destroy him only out of necessity. Eliza believed that had the situation been reversed, she'd have appreciated this sentiment. Nice to know your executioner didn't hate you on some unknown principle. However, thoughts like this might be evidence her brain was too twisted to understand the logic of others. Who among the condemned would find comfort in these reasons when their fate remained the same?

"I wouldn't mock you like that," she said. "I just needed someone to blame the robbery on." Eliza skipped the part about framing him for her murder. Now she speculated on whether her disappearance could be blamed on Michael. Some of the blood from her nose dotted the ground, leaving possible evidence of an abduction, but she didn't know how the dead boy fit into the narrative. Perhaps the police would think the two young lovers were performing some kind of séance when Bobby arrived and shot Michael down out of jealousy? It might work.

"Why did we really take the books?" Bobby asked. "Don't give me any more shit about resurrection. If you could manage that, our friend with the hole in his head wouldn't be a problem."

"You just went along with it to fuck me." Eliza understood the power pretty girls had over plain boys. She didn't feel any malice, just needed to quell his indignant tone.

"Well, we're both fucked now," Bobby said.

"The books are valuable. I know a collector who will pay a lot for them."

"And you thought you'd lock me in here? Call the police and report me with the stolen trash?"

When Eliza didn't respond, she saw Bobby understood it was worse than that.

"Someone would've come for you eventually," she said. "I would've made sure."

"After I spent the night with some corpses."

Outside, it had started to rain. Droplets slapped the tiled roof and echoed hollowly.

"You come from money, so your trouble isn't the kind you can tell Daddy about," Bobby said. "Must be bad if you were willing to seduce me."

"You've got a right to be angry over the money. People are buying your whole town, but this other thing is your own fault. I'm no great actress and you're no dullard. You allowed yourself to be deceived."

Bobby took the insult, and Eliza found him radiant in that moment, with his brow furrowed and teeth clenched.

"Feeling sorry for yourself because girls ignore you does nothing to improve your situation."

"What would you know about it? Hot little rich bitch who can have anyone she wants."

"Poor little hick who thinks so little of himself he can't get anybody. Grow up. Play the hand you're dealt. The reason girls won't fuck you isn't because you're ugly. Girls don't want to fuck you because you go around acting neutered by your circumstances. The same reason you never acted like a man until you got that gun in your hand."

Bobby looked over at the dead boy. "As opposed to him?"

Eliza wiped at her nostrils and came away with a line of blood trailing the back of her hand. "He's just some pussy-whipped fool. If that's what sex does to boys, you virgins are better off."

Insults were a poor idea, but Eliza couldn't help herself. Even trapped in this crypt with the gun trained on her, she couldn't stop the flood pouring from her mouth. Bobby might do anything. Beat her, rape her, gun her down for witnessing the murder, but she didn't believe any of that would happen. There was something about the boy, something essentially kind, that Eliza recognized was lacking in herself.

"Are you going to hurt me?" she asked.

"No, but you're coming with me."

"Where?"

"To sell off those books. Whatever you needed the money for, I need it more now."

Eliza shook her head. "You might as well shoot me."

"Don't be dramatic," Bobby said. "We go see this buyer of yours together. I get seventy percent. Don't argue. This isn't a negotiation."

"So I'm a hostage now?"

"If that's how you want to think of it. Don't try to run or fuck me over. I promise we'll go our separate ways after I've got my share."

And do what with it? Eliza thought. Run for the border like an outlaw in some dime Western? The severity of their predicament hadn't settled in. The boy said they'd go their separate ways, but Eliza knew he still expected this to morph into a romance. Young killers on the road like he was Starkweather. But that fantasy existed in another world without DNA evidence or GPS tracking. Bobby didn't understand that he'd abandoned any future freedom when he pulled that trigger.

"Where's the buyer?" he asked.

"Florida. A town outside of Jacksonville called Gladwell."

"We'll need transportation," Bobby said. "How were you planning on leaving?"

"Dad's car," she lied. No way Eliza could've disappeared and taken her father's car, but she didn't want to make this kidnapping any easier.

"Obviously I'm not taking you home," Bobby said. "I've got an idea where we can find some wheels."

No words were spoken over Michael's body. The pair locked the tomb's door and made their way across the cemetery. Eliza searched for the grave of Hazel Adkins. She didn't know the departed but had hidden a duffel bag beside the headstone earlier that evening with a change of clothes, a flashlight, her paperback copy of *Lonesome Dove*, and a butterfly knife she'd bought from a flea market in Louisiana. She needed that knife. It might be the only way she could get the pistol away from Bobby.

Eliza expected Bobby would search the bag before letting her have it, but he merely asked to see the contents. She slipped her hand inside, palmed the small blade, and showed him the rest of the bag's items, confident he could barely see in the darkness. As she rifled through the clothes, the legs from a pair of jeans fell out and hung like the entrails of a field-dressed deer.

"Satisfied?" she asked.

"Give me that T-shirt," Bobby said. "I've got blood on me."

The light rain washed their skin but made the blood-caked clothing hang sodden and heavy. Eliza tossed Bobby the long black T-shirt she'd packed to sleep in. The boy seemed reluctant to undress, as if she might charge in that brief moment of vulnerability. He ripped his bloody shirt overhead and discarded it in a single motion. Each arm slid into the new shirt one at a time, careful to make sure the pistol was always exposed.

"Are you going to watch me change?" Eliza asked.

Bobby turned his back to her. "I'll hear you coming if you try to sneak up on me."

Eliza wondered if that were true. If she moved slow, dragging her feet in the rain-slick grass, could she unsheathe the blade and slide it in before he turned? Did she have it in her to cut him? She'd certainly been willing to let him rot in jail until all hope or vitality left his life, so why not open his veins? Bobby didn't look like he had the resolve to take a life, but she'd seen him do it. Sure, pulling a trigger was more passive than twisting the knife, but either one extinguished a man.

In the end, Eliza changed her clothes. Bobby never peeked out of curiosity or concern for his own well-being.

Once she was dressed, Bobby asked for her phone.

"Why do you need my phone?"

"Don't play stupid."

She gave it to him. The boy tossed it into the pond. They stood watching the ripples expand from the place where it hit, then walked to the bikes. When they arrived, Bobby refused to let Eliza mount hers.

"Too easy to ride off from me," he said, and took his own bike by the handlebars.

"Why not leave yours too?" she asked.

"I need it for something," Bobby said.

CHAPTER SEVEN

HARLAN WINTER

The shop lay in complete disarray when I arrived. Even from the street, I saw the back door had been breached, the small glass panes in the upper window broken so that a hand might snake through and spring the lock. Despite the accumulating puddles, the fallen shards crunched underfoot as I stepped inside. The shelves weren't in terrible shape. I'd expected to find the display cases smashed like the door, but their locks had been picked with surprising skill. I took a quick inventory. A few charms and candles were missing, and an overturned mason jar of herbs spilled out onto the carpet, giving the room the warm scent of sage and peppermint. I never kept money in the register, but the robbers hadn't bothered tampering with it. Who would ransack the display cases and leave the register untouched? It wasn't until I noticed the beam of light leaking down the staircase that I even remembered to check my apartment. I took the stairs two at a time, leaning hard on the handrail as I climbed.

The kitchen had been raided. The fridge door left hanging open until my milk felt warm, and the flatware dumped from my counter drawers during the frantic searching. The living room appeared untouched. Quilts still folded on the couch. Cheap throw pillows I hated for their stiffness remained in their designated spots on the sofa. Most of the carnage was reserved for the bedroom and adjoining bathroom. The contents of my medicine cabinet had been raked into the sink below. Band-Aids, peroxide, and bottles of Advil collected in the basin, along with the remnants of hospital beard I'd failed to wash down the drain. The lid for the toilet tank lay across the bowl. I suppose someone might hide valuables in the commode, but I couldn't imagine why. I wanted to sit down on the linoleum and bury my head in my hands until the throbbing in my temples ceased. Instead, I made myself press on into the bedroom.

I knew my private collection was gone as soon as I saw the open closet door. Looking at the bare space, I hadn't realized what little room the irreplaceable books took up. The thief could've carried them off in a single grocery bag. I'd considered selling a few volumes before my dinner invitation. Now I had rent, hospital bills, and nothing set aside to sustain me.

I sat on the edge of the unmade bed and tried to control my breathing. Dr. McClain taught me a technique for weathering the worst visions. I performed the breathing exercises for another minute or two until I regained some semblance of composure. I knew who'd taken the books. I've never believed in coincidences, and even if there was the odd occurrence, I certainly didn't believe that I'd lost my most treasured possessions on the same night I'd been invited to dine with fellow occultists. The only thing that gave me pause about the coming confrontation was the poor plan. What weaker pretense to get me out of the apartment than the dinner party? Billings would've been better off robbing me that morning and saving the weak attempt at subterfuge.

The thought of armed robbery sent me back down into the shop for my gun. The hollow book remained in its familiar place behind the counter, but the pistol was missing. The few charms and candles felt like misdirection, but the gun was different. Its absence represented something I didn't yet understand. No matter. I had another. A long-barreled Smith & Wesson .357 hidden under my mattress.

I went upstairs, fetched the pistol, and headed outside to my car. It had finally stopped raining.

Earlier that night I'd detoured around Moss Street and taken the long way home. I hadn't wanted to go straight back to the house. If I was honest, I was afraid of the empty rooms. My furious state seemed like an invitation for Brandon's arrival, and I wanted to delay that for as long as possible. This time I charted the most direct route to the coven, cutting through the revitalized parts of downtown I usually avoided. When I rounded the corner at the boulevard, I saw someone sweeping up glass from the sidewalk. The storefront advertised one of the new boutiques whose name I hadn't bothered to learn. I did remember the ridiculous cartoon possum and the little gingham blouses on the mannequins in the window. The woman who owned the place, a middle-aged northerner with her chestnut hair piled atop her head in a knot and secured with something resembling chopsticks, worked the broom up and down the street. I pulled to the side of the road. She didn't look up at first, too occupied in her sweeping and busy lamenting the poor decision to move somewhere so uncivilized. Sure, it seemed like good prospects, taking a broken place and building it back up into something habitable. The sort of last adventure one hopes for in a world fully mapped, but considering the river rock someone hurled through the demolished window, I could tell she

wondered why bringing culture to such an unrefined and unapprecia-
tive bunch of mountain trash had ever seemed plausible.

I rolled down my window. "Excuse me."

The woman flinched as if the next stone might be meant for her
skull. She turned with the broom clasped tight like a weapon.

"I didn't mean to startle you," I said. "I see you've had some trouble."

"Oh, yes. A little bit." Her voice carried a hint of caution prompted
by the hour and the fact she was conversing with a stranger on a dark
street. Where she was from, random men didn't approach lone women
at night without suspicion.

"My name is Harlan Winter. I own the bookstore a few blocks over."
The introduction might do more harm than good. The woman would've
at least heard stories about the man who'd survived The Lighthouse.
After my time in the hospital, I was likely infamous.

"Yes," the woman said. "My apologies for not stopping by to introduce myself. I'm Dorothy Johnson. I'm from Vermont originally."

Her polite cadence obfuscated the fact we were talking in front
of a shattered window. I imagined Ms. Johnson had never encountered such a night. The elegant sweater she'd chosen for dirty work and
the expensive gold frames on her glasses telegraphed her prior life as a
comfortable early retiree. Maybe a little bored with book clubs and the
symphony but making do until some fool friend convinced her they'd
start a business in a forgotten corner of Appalachia.

"Did you call the police yet?" I asked.

"I did. They told me they'd be out to look at things as soon as they
could. I didn't know if I should clean up or not—you know, because
of evidence—but they told me I could just go ahead. If I'm being honest, and I hate to think this way, I really do, but they didn't seem to
take things very seriously." When I didn't respond, she rambled on. "I
mean, I'm sure that it's a small department and that they've got other

obligations, but now that I think of it, they didn't even take down all of my information."

"Ma'am, I've lived here all my life. I can promise you they don't give a rat's ass about your window." I exaggerated my pronunciation into "winda." A speech welled up inside me. An eager diatribe full of admonishments about how she'd moved to a wild place where self-reliance was paramount, and that if city folk planned to buy up half the property downtown, maybe they should've anticipated blowback from those people they'd bought out. If she'd bothered to read a little local history, she'd know this part of the country had long been a bastion of resistance against wealth. This was the land of the mine wars, of the Matewan Massacre and the Battle of Blair Mountain, where ten thousand union miners stood their ground for five days against government troops and US planes during the largest labor uprising in American history. Those miners had taken to the hills with nothing more than shotguns and deer rifles in defiance against strikebreakers, oppressive mine barons, and the law. The descendants of the men who'd fought and died on that mountain wouldn't let their home be usurped without some acts of guerrilla-influenced vandalism.

She didn't respond to the comment about the cops, and I decided there was no need for all my spite. She'd either adapt or make room for the next rich outsider. Meanwhile, my people would throw a few more stones, but it wouldn't change anything.

"Point is, ma'am, you're on your own out here. Did you happen to see who did it?"

Dorothy seemed hesitant to inform on her new neighbors. She looked up and down the street as if someone might overhear her.

"I just saw them riding away. There were two of them on bikes. One green mountain bike and one that looked like a girl's bike. It had a basket on the handlebars."

I imagined the pair speeding from my shop, their basket heavy with my stolen books. Why break this window? They hadn't taken anything from Dorothy's. What purpose did it serve?

"Did you tell this to the police?" I asked.

"No," she said, furrowing the heavy brows under her blonde bangs and gripping the broom tighter. "I figured I'd tell them everything when they arrived."

"The law's not coming tonight. Not for this. They may send someone tomorrow, but probably not. That's how things work here."

Dorothy's eyes widened behind the golden frames. "Oh, yes, sir. I'm finding out how things work around here. You bet."

"If they come back or you see them riding by again, you give me a call."

She looked suspicious of the gesture but took her iPhone from the pocket of her sweatpants and added my number to her contacts.

"We have to look out for each other here," I said. "Nobody else will."

I'd been concerned the line sounded too folksy, but Dorothy nodded in agreement. She seemed to be waiting on something further, perhaps for me to be a gentleman and sweep up the remaining glass on the sidewalk. Only I'd grown tired of the charade. Besides, I had places to be. I gave her a final nod, proclaimed, "Good evening," and rolled my window up as I drove off.

I parked in a vacant lot a block from Billings's place. I took the pistol from the glove box, checked the cylinder a final time, and shoved the gun into the back of my pants. As I leaned forward, I caught a glance of Brandon Flanders in the rearview mirror. The dead man sat in the center of the back seat, looking out the window. He'd appeared in my back seat once before. I'd been ferrying the body of a stranger and a woman I loved while the ghost accompanied their cold flesh as if reminding me of the possibility of some existence beyond the physical, a hope that something remains after consciousness winks out and the host expires. Dr. McClain helped reinstill my medical school training and the certainty that there was no room for the soul; no mysteries in the body once you take it apart, weigh, and measure each organ. I didn't know if I should be thankful for that return to logic. Considering it, I understood the appeal of folklore, superstition, and madness. Madness, most of all. How easy to just acquiesce to these visitations and befriend the ghost. A constant companion. A shadow self that would never leave, despite the inadequacies of your company. Some men might cherish the thought, but I kept pushing the spirit away.

"You got a plan?" I asked the ghost.

I was indulging in ways Dr. McClain warned could become a dangerous precedent, but I admit feeling relief at not being alone. In fact, the dead man's silence made me angrier. If Brandon was going to show himself, he might at least participate in the conversation.

"Nothing to say, huh?" I asked. "As useless now as ever before."

Our eyes connected in the rearview. We'd had moments like this in the hospital but only in the rare depths of my deepest delusions, when the doctors had to strap me down and pump me full of antipsychotics. Not that any drug succeeded in taking Brandon away. They only made me ambivalent to his presence. I broke my gaze and stepped out of the car. I'd expected the ghost to follow, but I walked alone up the slight hill. At the crest I saw Billings's house in the distance. All the downstairs lights were extinguished, but a single bulb burned in one of the upstairs windows. I'd knock on the front door and shove the pistol barrel in the mouth of whichever witch answered. I liked the sound of that plan, but something more subtle might get me further. Maybe the cops didn't come out for broken windows, but they'd shut down the interstate over an armed home invasion.

I opened the gate, crossed the yard, and went around to the back door. The wraparound porch circled most of the house. I climbed the steps quietly, moving in a heel-to-toe technique my uncle Abbott taught me. Uncle Abbott had been an expert burglar, and while he never offered much instruction that didn't involve the back of his hand, the stealthy walk proved efficient. The back entrance was reinforced with a screen door. I took a pocketknife from my jeans and cut a small slit in the mesh. After disengaging the screen door's lock, I went to work on the back door's bolt with a credit card. Amazing, the country people who didn't have dead bolts. I figured city folks would have multiple locks, but maybe they simply hadn't installed them yet.

The back door led me into the kitchen where Jeremiah Reynolds sat at the small table with a mug of heavily creamed coffee. He was still wearing his twill button-down shirt and chinos from dinner, but the slacks were rumpled and the shirt collar sagging. I didn't know how long he'd been waiting. It must have been a while. Reynolds didn't hear me as I crossed the tile floor. Closer, I saw a pair of white earbuds stuck in his ears. I raised the pistol, rolled back the hammer, and placed the barrel against the base of his neck. Using my mutilated hand, I reached forward and plucked the tiny speaker from his ear. A little voice squeaked. No doubt Billings pontificating about some supernatural matter on their podcast. I sat the earbud on the tabletop beside the steaming mug.

"Don't shoot," Reynolds said. He kept his voice low and calm, as if the situation were not entirely foreign to him.

"What are you doing up this hour?" I asked.

"Waiting on the girl. She hasn't come home yet."

I wondered why he cared. It wasn't his daughter. If Billings could go to sleep without seeing her home safe, why did the old man bother sitting up like a worried mother?

"Where'd she go?" I asked.

"Out with some boy. If you're going to hurt someone, I'd ask that you leave the women be." Reynolds tried to crane his head back and look at me, but I stopped him by pressing the barrel down harder.

"All I want is my property. I get that back and no one gets hurt."

"What property are you referring to?"

"As if you don't know."

"I assure you that I do not."

"I came home to find my shop and apartment robbed. No money's gone, but several books from my collection are missing. The sort of books your coven would be interested in."

"We didn't have anything to do with that," Reynolds said.

"You think I'm that stupid?" I asked. "My books just happened to disappear during your dinner party? I'm supposed to buy that kind of coincidence?"

"If it's so ridiculous," Reynolds asked, "why wouldn't we have a better plan? Do you think we're simpletons? Billings has bigger designs for you than a couple books."

"He wants to exploit me on the podcast."

Reynolds snorted. "He wants to bring you into the fold."

The possibility had occurred to me at dinner. The whole proceeding felt like an audition, the other members appraising me to see if I fit into the little group. The idea repulsed me. After what I'd seen with The Lighthouse, nothing seemed less appealing than orienting every aspect of my life around their community. I was ready to tell Reynolds all this when a creaking echoed through the house. Bare feet on stairs, a man's lazy weight shifting as he staggered across the den. I pressed the barrel against Reynolds's head, hoping that the gesture might communicate what my necessary silence could not. The footsteps came closer. I kept the pistol on Reynolds as Billings materialized from the darkness of the dining room like a ship charting its shoreward course through morning fog. Just the shape of the man first, then a broad chest clad in a plaid house robe, arms deep in the patch pockets. Billings flipped on the light and squinted as his eyes were assaulted by the brightness. He remained calm. No screams or threats or other theatrics. He kept his hands in the pockets of the robe and spoke with caution.

"You don't need that gun, Mr. Winter. Whatever is going on here, we can resolve it peacefully."

"Where are my books?" I asked.

"I have no idea what you mean. Please take that gun off my friend."

"I'm getting tired of repeating myself," I said. "I left dinner and came home to my place robbed. Books from my private collection were gone. Books only people like you would know about."

"I'm going to take my hands out of my pockets and sit down."

He removed his hands and grasped the chair at the head of the table. I stiffened, waiting to see if he'd make a grab for the gun, but he only pulled the chair out and sat down. I pulled out my own chair and sat beside Reynolds, keeping the gun above the table.

"Each of us was in your presence all night," Billings said. "How could we have robbed you?"

"What about your daughter?" I asked.

"What are you implying?"

"She wasn't at dinner. Mr. Reynolds tells me she's out on a date."

"You're accusing my daughter?" Billings said.

"Someone also broke the windows of a shop downtown. The owner saw two people riding away on bikes. Does your daughter ride a bike with a handlebar basket?"

I saw alarm in Billings's eyes. When he didn't respond, I raised the gun. "She'll be home eventually. We're gonna sit here and wait."

Reynolds grabbed the mug off the table and threw lukewarm coffee in my face. I blocked most with my arm, letting the coffee saturate my shirtsleeve. I kept my grip on the gun as Reynolds swung the empty mug. The blow glanced off my left shoulder. I brought the pistol around, striking Reynolds across the chin with the barrel. Bone and teeth clacked. Reynolds fell from his chair and rolled onto the floor, blood pouring from the gash in his cheek. He spit out a yellow fragment of tooth. I found myself surprised he didn't wear dentures.

I turned the gun on Billings. "Let me check on him," he said.

The commotion had likely woken the women. They might be waiting on the staircase in their nightgowns, perhaps whispering to dispatch about the marauder ruining the men downstairs. The desire to flee rose like floodwaters, but I couldn't go without finishing things with Billings.

"Tell me where she is, or I go upstairs and we question the women," I said. I didn't think he'd leave Reynolds's side, but it was a calculated bluff I hoped he wouldn't call.

"Promise you won't hurt anyone else. Especially my daughter."

"If you lie to me, I promise to hurt you."

Billings raised Reynolds's head and stared into his eyes. The old man gripped his hand and told him to go.

"I'll be fine," he said. "Get him away from here before the girls come down."

"You know where she is?" I asked Billings.

"I have a tracker on her phone."

I wasn't exactly surprised by this. Fathers can be overly protective of their daughters, but this one had gone on to bed while the older man waited up. Apparently Billings wanted to know where his daughter was but didn't care enough to fetch her when she stayed out too late.

"Give it to me," I said.

"Not a chance. I'm not leaving her alone with you."

Another sound somewhere off in the house. There was no time to argue. Besides, I had the gun. Billings wouldn't present any problems that a pistol-whipping couldn't solve.

"Let's go."

Billings gave Reynolds a final caress across his bloody cheek and rose to follow me out the back door.

CHAPTER EIGHT

BOBBY WISE AND ELIZA BILLINGS

Bobby called Ryan because the boy was the only person in his life who came within a mile of being considered a friend. It was nearly two in the morning, so Bobby expected some resistance when he requested to come over. Ryan's father might object to company, or he'd be chastised for getting them out of bed with a phone call, but Ryan answered without a hint of sleep in his voice. The television blared in the background. An action flick with explosions and automatic-weapon fire Ryan talked over, crunching on a late-night snack while he listened.

"The old man's off on a bender," Ryan said. "The door's unlocked."

They walked side by side out of the cemetery, but Bobby couldn't make the girl follow the whole way on foot. Ryan lived several miles on the other side of town. A decent ride even on the bike. Bobby mounted and offered Eliza his hand. She wrapped her arms around his waist. The closeness would've tantalized Bobby just hours before. Feeling her hands on him now, he thought only about the way she might reach for his throat or the pistol stuck down the front of his pants. Risks he'd have to take. He steered the bike down the hill and across town.

They were nearly a mile out of the graveyard when Eliza lay her head against Bobby's back and cried. Acquiescing to the tears felt like offering Bobby a victory, but thinking of Michael abandoned in the crypt had bested her. She didn't cry out of love. She cried because the boy died young, never knowing he left anything of worth behind, yet she was still determined to rid herself of his child. There was no guilt in this decision. If anything, her resolve felt more assured. What child needed a woman like her as a mother? Had Michael lived, the baby would've been no better off with its father. The unborn's only hope was a decent foster family, but a happy home in state custody remained too rare a possibility. She was still going through with her plan, and it was best Michael hadn't survived to know that.

As the tears subsided, Eliza considered plunging the knife into Bobby's neck. They moved fast, the bike swerving into the turns with grace despite her added weight. The crash would be hard, but she'd survive. Skinned knees and sprains. Perhaps a single broken bone. Only then, she'd be riding in an ambulance. Lying in a hospital bed, waiting on the doctor to release her to detectives and her father. Both parties requiring her story. There was also the matter of the cutting. Eliza couldn't do it. Maybe if he menaced her in some way or if he pulled the pistol again, but she couldn't murder the boy.

Ryan lived on the opposite side of a defunct set of railroad tracks and up a winding road at the far end of Grant Hollow. The tracks were once well traveled with coal trains moving nearly a thousand tons each night down from the tipple at the top of the mountain. That was Coopersville's past. The derelict tracks had sat unused for nearly a quarter of a century. Rust overtook the idle rails, and the wooden ties broke up into splintered remnants unable to bear the weight of even a modest load. Bobby rode over these rotten planks with the witch gripping him tight.

Civilization disappeared as they turned up the hollow. Even the yellow lines on the weathered asphalt faded into nonexistence. This road represented an attempt to defy the wilderness, and yet wilderness endured around them. Something about an outpost not susceptible to change reminded Eliza there were places where the new money could not yet venture. If the pair closed their eyes and ignored the busted blacktop, only the rustle of wind in the trees and the nocturnal song of crickets would remain.

Off to the left side of the road, a few trailers clung close to the mountainside, nearly hidden by the low-hanging canopy of trees. Ryan lived in the last trailer of the row. A blue single-wide with absent under-pinning and golden shutters. A stack of cinder blocks led up to the screened front door. Heavy quilts sufficing for drapes blocked any light from shining through the front windows, but they could hear the drone of the television. The sounds of war that dominated Bobby's call were replaced by the screams of a young girl doubtlessly being mutilated during a drive-in horror show. They left the bike on its kickstand by the improvised steps but took the basketful of books. Bobby looked at Eliza. She had her head hung down, refusing to meet his eyes. Embarrassment still lingered from the tears. Anything might await them inside, so she fortified herself by touching the hidden blade.

"Do we need to talk about your behavior in here?" Bobby asked.

"You're only in charge because you've got that gun," Eliza said. "Don't think for a second you're some kind of real man."

"Take a good look around," Bobby said. "This isn't your world any-more, princess. Keep your mouth shut and let me do the talking. Ryan's the kind of guy who'd eat us if he ran out of deer steaks."

There was truth in what he said. Eliza was out of her element. Not because she'd never seen poverty. There'd been plenty of shithole apartments or tired farmhouses with the coven, but she knew this was a different kind of place. Here she had the reputation of money, and there was nothing some poor boys desired more than revenge on daughters of the rich.

Eliza's nose began dripping again. She tasted blood filling the cracks between her front teeth and canines.

"So long as he eats you first," she said.

Bobby felt his cock stir. The defiance was sexy. He was considering some witty retort when the screen door whined open. Ryan leaned out, holding a bag of Fritos in one hand and the television remote in the crumb-dusted other.

"Get on in here," he said. "I'm missing Joe Bob and Darcy."

The trailer smelled of fried food, a tinge of old butter and sautéed onions mingling with mildewed laundry and the ghost of some carcinogen like black mold. The living room made up the majority of the space and consisted of a single oxblood couch; a coffee table covered in crushed beer and soda cans; and a fifty-inch TV, where Jason Voorhees stalked a brunette in tiny khaki shorts. No lights aside from the ambient glow of the television. Looking at the squalor, Eliza thought the boy had a right to hate her.

Ryan sat back down on the couch, shoveled a palmful of Fritos into his mouth, and waited on an explanation. Bobby didn't know where to begin, but it didn't matter. Ryan was fixated on the girl. Eliza noticed but didn't return his stare, just stood looking over the false hardwood floors, curious where the roaches scuttled when assaulted by light.

"What can I do for the witch of Coopersville High?" Ryan asked. He crammed more Fritos into his mouth. The crunching of chips was overcome by the screams of the Final Girl on the television.

"We need to ask a favor," Bobby said. "It's important."

"Looks more like an emergency. Before coming over, you asked where my dad was. Now you're here, looking scared half to death, and the little witch's nose might be broken. You want to explain?"

Eliza wasn't in a mood to be toyed with by the little shit. "If Bobby's really a friend, you'll help us. If not, we'll be on our way."

"This witch speak for you?" Ryan asked. He turned the volume down on the television. Shadows hid his face, but Bobby caught glimpses of Ryan's eyes when the TV flashed. They were hard and flat. The same eyes Ryan had possessed when he cut the deal for Bobby's bike.

"We need transportation and a little cash," Eliza said. "If you help us, I'll see that you're compensated."

Ryan scarfed down more Fritos. "What kind of compensation? If you think I'm gonna let you take cash and keys without knowing what I stand to gain, you're very mistaken."

Bobby looked to Eliza. He didn't know how much more to reveal, but the girl took up the conversation. "I've got something rare and a buyer waiting on delivery. If you lend us some wheels and starting cash, we'll cut you in. Twenty percent."

Bobby set the chips aside. He stood and walked around the coffee table, his knee brushing against the cans and sending them toppling together before they spilled on the floor. He kicked them away with the toe of his sneaker.

"You overestimate your situation. A girl like you has resources. Money and Daddy's car. But by the look of you, I'd say those aren't options. You've got traces of blood in your hair and dirt under your nails. Not to mention both of you are sober despite the fact this lovesick fool traded his bike for some premium bud. Now, I can't diagnose what trouble, but it's bad. That means if you want money and a ride, we're partners. A partner, even a silent one, gets half."

Bobby looked at Eliza for protest. She stood with her fingers curled into fists but made no counteroffer. The little shit had them bested, and she knew it. Ryan waited on some further negotiation and, when none came, only nodded.

"What's the item, and how far do you have to go to deliver it? Not being nosy, just hoping for some perspective."

"A few books," Bobby said. "We're going to Florida."

Ryan scratched his throat and whistled through his rotten teeth. "The only ride I can offer isn't licensed. It'll get you only so far before the law catches up with you. Let me think a minute." Ryan turned his attention to the television. Jason had the brunette cornered. She cowered behind a bed while the slasher hacked at the mattress with a machete.

"Think you can push to North Carolina tonight?" Ryan asked.

"We can make the Carolinas," Bobby said. Neither was sure they could make it so far. The pair felt tired to the bones but would push if it meant placing some miles between them and Coopersville.

"My cousin's got a place you can shack up for the night in Bluebird, just south of Charlotte. You leave Dad's truck there, and he'll hook you up with a bed, some clothes, and fresh wheels. All I have in cash is three hundred dollars. That enough to get you started?"

"It should be," Eliza said. "Thank you."

"Shit, don't thank me yet." Ryan went into the kitchenette and took a key ring with a single golden key from a hook beside the refrigerator. "Come out back," he said, and held the screen door open.

They crossed the high grass of the small lot and walked behind the trailer. A blue Ford F-150 from the early 2000s sat parked in a patch of dead grass. The sidewalls were eaten away with rust, the vinyl seats ripped and sun bleached. The headliner hung looser than a grandmother's tit. Bobby wasn't sure the rust bucket would start. Eliza couldn't hide her disgust. She scoffed and shook her head until hair lashed around her ears.

"This thing won't make it to Virginia," she said.

Ryan patted the hood as if the truck were an old horse. "She doesn't look like much but runs good. Problem is with the license. Nothing is current, but you should be fine as long as you go the speed limit. Cousin Frank will have something better waiting."

Ryan took five fifty-dollar bills, two twenties, and a ten from the pocket of his jeans.

"Remember, this is a loaner. You leave it with Cousin Frank. Now, our final bit of business. What's my return on this?"

"Right around five thousand," Eliza said. Bobby knew the number was a low-ball fabrication but played along. Neither his posture nor face telegraphed any falsehood.

Ryan gave them the key. "Last thing. I need you to bust my lip. It's still Dad's truck. He'll do a lot worse if he finds out I just handed it over."

"What if he reports it stolen?" Eliza asked.

"My dad ain't talking to the police. Seriously now, bust my lip."

Eliza punched Ryan in the mouth before Bobby could react. The quick shot snapped his head, staggering the boy as he took a step backward to keep from collapsing. He spit a stream of blood, wiped his mouth, and gave a smile.

"Nice one, bitch," he said. "Not as good as the one that smashed your nose, but not too bad."

Eliza kept her hands balled into fists but didn't rise to the bait. Bobby took her by the wrist. Her muscles tensed with his touch, a spasm shooting through her arm as she resisted the urge to jerk it free, but she allowed herself to be led to the truck. Bobby opened her door. Eliza climbed in with the bike's wicker basket full of books resting on her lap.

"The bike is in the front yard," Bobby said. "This cousin of yours. Is he really going to help?"

"Think I'd fuck you over?"

"I'm just realizing you're not my friend."

A pearl of blood leaked from the cut in Ryan's lip. "I don't have friends, Bobby. I also don't screw over those I do business with. It's bad for future prospects."

Ryan extended his hand and Bobby shook it. The grip was hard and dry, with reptilian calluses on the boy's fingertips. Bobby climbed up into the truck cab. The engine fought hard to turn over. It sputtered, gears grinding before the pistons fired and the motor roared with life. A plume of burned oil spewed from the exhaust in a black cloud. Bobby cranked the windows up and pulled out of the driveway and around the trailer. A shimmy rocked the cab as they traversed the poorly paved road, and the alignment drifted to the left. Bobby kept the truck steady even in the curves. They went a mile before Eliza spoke up.

"Your friend is a real piece of shit."

"I don't have any friends."

Bobby expected sarcasm or some other remark like the ones she'd given him in the crypt, but Eliza didn't say anything for a long moment. She'd underestimated the boy's plight, considered it all some sort of melancholic exaggeration, but he really did seem entirely alone. Eliza knew that feeling. The same loneliness had filled her even in the bough of her favorite chestnut tree.

"You really traded your bike for some weed?" she asked.

"Yes."

"Why?"

"I wanted to impress you. Show you I had a hookup for the good stuff."

The closest thing Bobby had seen yet to shame crossed Eliza's brow. It was only a flash, a brief instant where she lost the poker-faced control of her expressions, but it was there. Bobby saw it.

"Well, do you still have it?" she asked.

"Are you serious?"

"Very. It's been a hard night. Can you smoke and drive?"

"Don't know. I've never tried."

"Well, let's spark one up."

Bobby went into his pocket and pulled out the tiny cellophane baggie with the pre-rolled joints. He passed it to Eliza, who took a joint from the bag and straightened it by licking the paper. Bobby fished the lighter from his pocket and lit the joint as she leaned over to accept the flame. The skunk odor had instantaneously filled the cab when Eliza opened the plastic, but the lit joint created a noxious cloud that stole Bobby's breath, enveloping him even after he cracked the window. Eliza pressed the joint to Bobby's lips, letting him suck it pinched between her fingers so he could concentrate on the road. All fear dissipated with the next hit. Suddenly the road felt full of promise, their journey not destined to be one of doom and reprisals. Pleasure filled Bobby, and he heard himself cast out a smoke-filled cackle.

"That was one hell of a punch," he told her.

Eliza didn't laugh, but the compliment did elicit a grin.

CHAPTER NINE

HARLAN WINTER

We found Eliza's bike in the cemetery after following the tracking app on Barney's phone. Apparently the device periodically sent updates of her location, and the last report came from somewhere within the Memorial Gardens Cemetery. I drove while Barney sat hunched over, scrutinizing the screen and whispering something akin to prayer. The car gate was closed at the entrance, so we left the vehicle and walked out among the tombstones. Barney sloshed through the mud with the phone held high like a conduit to God as he turned about in the maze of monuments, hoping for an updated message to narrow our search.

I saw the bike first. An old Schwinn outfitted with high, curved handlebars and a wide seat that looked custom made for a rider suffering from hemorrhoids. You'd never guess the antiquated bike belonged to a young girl. Barney knelt beside it, wrapped his hands around the fenders, and rested his head on the seat. I surveyed our surroundings. No other living souls among the graves. The wet grass underfoot threatened to swallow my shoes, and the slope down toward the pond became more slurry than sod. Looking at the placid waters, a bad feeling hit me.

"Anything out of the ordinary about that bike?" I asked.

"She had a little wicker basket on the handlebars. It's gone."

"I think I know what happened to the phone."

Barney rested his elbows on the handlebars. Watching the tires sink in the soft mud, I didn't think the bike would hold his weight. Hard rain had tilled the ground until the entire acreage of earth threatened to collapse into one communal grave.

"What about the phone?"

"Is that tracker waterproof?" I asked, nodding at the pond.

The exertion of hiking across the cemetery had turned Barney's neck pink under the collar of his polo. Now, with the color drained from his face, he looked as pale as the nearest cross.

"Jesus," he finally uttered. The choice surprised me. I hadn't expected a witch to take the Lord's name in vain.

"I think you'd better tell me about this boy she went out with," I said. "Know much about him?"

"Not really. She'd been seeing somebody from summer school but told me things ended."

Even childless, I couldn't understand a father who didn't know more about his daughter's boyfriends. If she'd been mine, I'd have brought the young gentleman into the house and made sure he understood the proper etiquette for courting my daughter. Barney's face told me he regretted not doing that exact thing.

I turned on the flashlight he'd given me and traced it along the path winding around the pond. It didn't take long to find the first discarded article of clothing. A single pair of socks still wound together in a tight ball. Tiny and blue, with little purple polka dots. I thought about slipping them into my pocket and saving Barney the added panic, but something stopped me. Would they still be mated this way if she'd pulled them off? This wasn't someone undressing. I sniffed them and smelled fabric softener. The socks were not only clean, but freshly laundered. Likely spilled from a bag where they'd been tucked away with other changes of clothes. I expected Brandon to appear, as he had during my days investigating The Lighthouse, and offer some crucial information, but the rest of the dead must've kept him at bay.

I put the socks in my pocket, left Barney distraught with the bike, and followed the path around the pond. A few muddy footprints led me away from the water. I was about to abandon my search when the flashlight traced over something reflective. I walked toward the flickering shine and felt glass crunch underfoot. One of the panes from the nearby mausoleum had been knocked out. I recalled the broken glass at my shop and the shattered window from the outsider's storefront.

Shining my flashlight inside the mausoleum, I saw a leg extending from behind the caskets. The crooked appendage was clad in light-wash denim. A black Nike high-top with a dark-red swoosh adorned the only visible foot. Based on the attire, it wasn't one of the corpses interred decades ago.

"Barney," I called. "You need to see this."

It didn't take us long to get the chain off the door. I'm proficient at picking locks, and the mechanism had already been weakened by the previous occupants. Barney pulled the door open and was the first inside. I would've restrained him had it been a girl's foot, but I didn't mind him laying eyes on the boyfriend. Barney stood over the body and covered his mouth with a dirty hand. Medical training wasn't necessary to recognize the gunshot wound. A sizable hole gaped in the back of the boy's head. I rolled him over with the toe of my shoe.

"This Eliza's boy?" I asked.

"Maybe." Barney didn't take his hand away. Just spoke through his fingers.

"Well, these candles are from my shop. She's been in here with him."

"She wouldn't do this," Barney said, shaking his head.

"He didn't blow his own head off. There's no gun left behind."

"She doesn't have a gun."

"There was one missing from my shop."

Barney gritted his teeth so hard the enamel creaked. He shook his head. "I said she wouldn't do this."

"Maybe he was trying to hurt her."

Barney grasped his hair with both hands and pulled hard, as if freeing the fibers from his scalp might remedy the mess. He blew out a long breath and muttered words I couldn't hear.

"If she did it," he finally said, "it was because she had to do it."

I let him have that. Family shouldn't have to know the harm their loved ones are capable of committing. One of my few regrets was letting my father know what I'd done to Brandon. He'd trained me in the ways of inflicting pain, but I still felt that there was more pity than pride when he learned I wounded the boy. A little sadness that rage was another of my poor inheritances.

"We better call the police."

"We can't do that," Barney said.

"The bullet came from my gun. I have to report it."

"You're gonna report the gun stolen. That absolves you. You don't have to tell anyone about this. We lock up and leave everything as it is. If they ever find the boy, you're in the clear."

Cold even for a father. I wondered if Barney considered the parents of the dead kid at our feet. They'd wonder why their son never came home and seek him with the same fervor Barney had searched for Eliza. The body might not be found for years, but love wouldn't let them stop. Oaths would be made to find the missing and more lives lost to this night.

"Leave the police out of this," Barney said. "We find her together and get the full story of what happened here. You get your books back and anything else you want. If I have it, it's yours."

The coven didn't seem wealthy. Any money had probably been used as a down payment on the house. Billings had moved in just in time. It was respectable property, and real estate costs in Coopersville were only increasing. I was going to lose my apartment eventually, but I didn't want the house.

"If we find her, I get the books back. Promise to do that, and I'll help."

"I swear on my life."

I'd never made a covenant while standing over a dead man but decided no vow could be more sacred. I extended my hand and Barney shook it.

It didn't take long to put things back as we'd found them. I hadn't touched much but was careful to wipe down the lock and places where I might've grasped the door. Barney took the bike. I was concerned it wouldn't fit in the trunk, but we managed. Driving down the hill, I asked about Eliza.

"Where would she go if she was in trouble?"

"Home. I'd help her with anything."

A typical father's answer. I needed to break through that. "But what if she wanted to keep you from knowing something to protect you. Where would she go?"

"It's my job to protect her," he said. After a long moment, he sighed. "But I'm not sure. Maybe her mother's."

"Can you call her?"

"She's not the sort who'd understand this situation. She'd call the police first thing."

"Any friends?"

"She's new here."

As we descended the hill and turned toward town, Brandon appeared in my back seat again. His head lay against the middle seat cushion, resting as though he'd grown drowsy from the night's drive. The constant blood was still present on his upper lip, but the drip was less pronounced. His hands were clasped together in his lap with the fingers intertwined. I tried to keep my eyes on the road, but my gaze kept drifting back to the spirit.

Another case together. Another trip into the unknown to find the lost.

II

A Box of Spiders

CHAPTER TEN

ELIZA BILLINGS AND BOBBY WISE

They drove through the night. Bobby had been fighting sleep ever since they crossed through the East River Mountain Tunnel. Over a mile of subterranean road that ran beneath the last of West Virginia's mountains before depositing travelers into Rocky Gap, Virginia. The tunnel terrified Eliza. Its burning lamps couldn't suppress her fear of the absolute darkness the lights kept at bay or the million pounds of earth above them. No structures of concrete and steel could withstand that relentless geological pressure. Eventually the struts would buckle, the foundation crack, and the mountain collapse upon the commuters like the falling sky in a children's fable. The tunnel reminded Eliza of a documentary she once saw about the destruction of Pompeii. Ask the fossilized dead who'd built their city in the shade of that volcano about acts of hubris. If one could question those reduced to dust while baking bread or calcified standing in the street, they'd tell you plenty about the foolish nature of men.

Bobby watched as Eliza closed her eyes and held her breath. He steered the car with one hand and reached for her with the other. Eliza almost pulled away, but Bobby's touch was comforting. With her eyes closed, it didn't matter who was holding her. His thumb stroked the back of her wrist. Neither spoke until they were out of the artificial light and back onto the darkness of the road. It wasn't until they passed a sign declaring VIRGINIA IS FOR LOVERS that Eliza pulled free.

At first light, they stopped at a gas station for fuel and supplies. Eliza needed the bathroom but didn't want to ask permission to piss. She climbed out of the car and extended her hand.

"Give me some money. I'll pay for the gas while you pump."

Bobby studied her face for signs of betrayal. Stopping offered a thousand opportunities for escape. Eliza might beg the clerk on duty for help, or simply barricade herself in the bathroom until he drove on alone rather than make a scene. Bobby didn't understand what the girl was running from yet, but their relationship felt more symbiotic than one of kidnapper and captive. At least, he hoped this was true. The girl was smarter than him, and he hadn't forgotten the night's lies. Even holding hands in the tunnel could be fabricated weakness meant to throw him off guard.

Bobby peeled off three twenties from Ryan's roll. He slapped them into Eliza's palm. "You got five minutes to pay and piss."

"Or you'll leave without me?"

Bobby didn't answer. Eliza smiled, pleased with herself for reminding him she held some cards. "I'll be right back."

"Buy me some iced coffee. Maybe a Red Bull."

Bobby filled the tank with unleaded. Inside, Eliza paced the few aisles. The man behind the counter had watched her with rheumy eyes as she prepaid for the gas. He was obviously the owner, and the sort of weathered geriatric who asked young girls for their smiles in supermarkets. He might help her escape, but the books were still in the car. Besides, Eliza felt confident in her ability to steer Bobby. He'd liked holding her hand, and something about his actions in the tunnel reminded her of a braver boy who'd kissed her inside a haunted house one October night. The surprising touch spoke of a deeper well of confidence than she'd anticipated, but Eliza could control Bobby. As long as she kept her head, this was something she could ride all the way to freedom.

Eliza grabbed two Red Bulls, an iced coffee, a pack of teriyaki beef jerky, some salt-and-vinegar chips, cherry Twizzlers, and a giant bag of candied fruit slices. Their breakfast for the road. It was still over a hundred miles to North Carolina and the refuge of Cousin Frank.

Out the window, a police cruiser pulled in beside the pumps. Eliza slammed cash down on the counter and told the old man to keep her change.

Bobby replaced the nozzle as the highway patrol pulled in. The cop parked on the other side of the island of pumps and climbed out. A tall young officer with the standard wide-brimmed patrol hat and black Oakley sunglasses. He smacked chewing gum and wiped at the thin mustache on his upper lip as he walked toward Bobby. The officer's eyes couldn't be seen behind the shades, but Bobby felt the hidden stare evaluating him. Why might this young boy in the battered truck with an out-of-state license plate be filling up so early in the morning? Why did he look so tired, sweaty, and nervous? The pistol in the back of Bobby's jeans felt heavy. His hands froze around the handle of the nozzle as he hung it back on the pump.

When the door opened, Eliza came walking fast across the distance. She saw the way Bobby stared at the cop. The look of perplexed surprise on his face that screamed out suspicion. The officer hadn't noticed yet, but in just a moment he'd recognize the way the boy glared at him.

Eliza knew Bobby had the pistol. She'd told him to put it in the glove box, but the idiot wouldn't hear it. Retaining the firearm constituted all his authority.

Eliza saw the cop recognize he was being watched. Bobby saw as well. She widened her stride, stretching her legs and moving as fast as she could without running. Perhaps she imagined it, but Eliza thought she saw Bobby reaching behind him, fingers groping for the butt of the revolver. She wrapped her arms around Bobby and buried her head in his chest.

"They didn't have any of those lattes you like, babe." Eliza looked up at him with falsified teenage lust and took his hands. "You give me the keys. I'll drive a bit."

Bobby handed them over. Eliza kissed him on the mouth. She could feel his desire. His hands sliding around her waist, his neck bending and transforming what could've been only a peck on the lips into something languid and deep. Still, Bobby kept his mouth tight. He understood this wasn't the real second chance at a kiss she'd promised. This was only farce for the cop and made the sting of her prior lies more stringent. Eliza pulled away with a mixture of warning and apology in her eyes. The cop watched them. Just two dumb kids in love—or at least a state of teenage infatuation that would suffice for love. He tipped his campaign hat and went into the station. Bobby walked around the car, climbed in the passenger side, and sat quietly while Eliza adjusted the driver's seat.

They traveled in silence, but Eliza felt his disapproval. It was another ten miles before Bobby spoke up.

"You didn't need to do that," he said.

"You were seconds away from throwing down on that trooper like Wyatt fucking Earp."

The comment wounded him. Did she really think him that stupid? If she had just apologized for the kiss, the hopes he carried could be discarded. Why couldn't he rid himself of them? Why did he still feel these embers of desire for a girl who'd tricked and used him? When would he stop viewing The Flinch as a burden and appreciate its warnings?

"You couldn't think of anything else to do? I thought you were supposed to be smart."

Eliza shook her head. So much vitriol over a hard-on. It surprised her, the way a man could hate and want you simultaneously. She'd never felt that mix of arousal and disgust. Perhaps it was something unique to boys? Michael was the first to unleash that frustration, but she'd seen flashes of it in other men. Some of them far too old to pursue a girl her age. Few ever acted on it, but there was a dangerous undertow flowing beneath certain men's desires. A resentment because their longing acknowledged a hidden vulnerability and reminded them what they wanted might be out of reach. That was where things lay between her and Bobby.

"It was just a kiss," she said, aware of the stupidity of the comment. Barely deflowered, Eliza already knew it was never just a kiss. Not for boys like Bobby, who'd never even dreamed about the touch of a girl like her. "Grow up."

"We're gonna establish some rules," Bobby said. "No more decisions unless I make them. No more going places without me. You need to stop and rest? You need to piss? We do it when and where I approve. Understood?"

"Yes, sir."

———

After consuming most of the junk food and jerky, Eliza pulled over at a barbecue truck just inside the North Carolina line. They sat at one of the three picnic tables and ate pulled-pork sandwiches slathered in golden mustard sauce with sides of baked beans and vinegar-soaked collard greens, letting the sweet woodsmoke from the multiple grills envelop them. They were the only customers.

Bobby was surprised by Eliza's appetite. She ate ravenously and didn't mind sucking sauce from her fingers or spooning heaping plastic fork loads of beans into her already-chewing mouth. Bobby ate sparingly, afraid that mixing meat into his drowsy state would have him asleep before they arrived. Trust was growing, but no way was he going to sleep while she drove. Not with them so close to Cousin Frank's.

"Do you really trust Ryan?" Eliza asked.

"What do you mean?" Bobby replied.

Eliza licked a sticky finger. "He looked like a liar. I've never known someone could actually look like a liar."

Something untrustworthy did secrete off Ryan. Something unseen but felt, the way a dog smells sickness in an ill body.

"What if we just drive on?" she said. "It's not that much farther to Florida. I'll drive another few hours while you sleep. Afterwards we'll trade off."

But Eliza could already see the way Bobby bristled at the suggestion. It wasn't that she was wrong. Eliza understood that. It was that she'd suggested it, and Bobby was suspicious of anything she suggested.

"Look, I won't ask you to trust me," she said. "All I'm saying is we don't trust that little shit."

Bobby lay his plastic fork down on the foam tray. "We stop and get the new car. We sleep a few hours. We shower and change out of these clothes. I'll still get you to Florida in record time."

There was reasoning in her suggestion, but Bobby knew why he wasn't listening. It wasn't just establishing authority. There was a need to prolong the inevitable. Eliza's journey ended after the books were sold, but his own began there. The girl hadn't shot a boy. She could move back into life. He would have to find a place where the murder couldn't follow. Bobby wasn't ready to face that alone. Not yet. He needed more time to consider what came next.

They tossed their trays and went back on the road.

———

They hit Bluebird, North Carolina, before noon. It was the kind of town where kids grew up plotting their escape, the main thoroughfare only a few dusty streets occupied by a defunct theater, a market, the courthouse, a diner, two competing law offices, and not much else. The sort of place that tolerated its single bar and considered two churches a sign of the population's diversity. Bobby should've hated the way it reminded him of Coopersville, but honestly, it made him nostalgic for his youth before the outsiders moved in. Eliza had seen too many places to bother noticing much of Bluebird. After so many years on the road, only extreme examples penetrated her apathy. She did wonder if the local pharmacy carried the drugs she needed. There was little money left in Ryan's roll, and a southern, small-town pharmacist likely wouldn't offer the sort of charity she required, but desperation kept her mind occupied on the possibility.

The pair followed Ryan's directions up a curvy road that declined from asphalt to gravel to dirt. Within another mile, the dirt reduced to a quagmire of mud created by an overflowing creek that ran parallel along the path. In the distance, they saw the double-wide trailer and collapsing tobacco barn of Cousin Frank's property. A small corral had been constructed out of split railing, and two horses—a palomino and a gray mare—circled inside the confines. The man sat outside on his porch, a sharecropper-style hat pulled low over his eyes and his muck boots kicked up on the porch rail, where they dripped some amalgamation of clay and horseshit. The sleeves of his work shirt were rolled up past the elbows, exposing the mural of tattoos that covered his forearms. At their approach, Cousin Frank pushed the hat brim up with the index finger of his right hand, squinted in their direction, and rubbed the back of his neck. Eliza goaded the truck through the high mud like a stubborn mule, pumping the gas and feeling the tires slosh through the soup until the treads bit into the solid ground below. Cousin Frank descended the stairs and gestured for them to roll the windows down.

"Gonna get mired in this shit," he said. Closer, Bobby could see the man wore a heavy gray mustache and long sideburns that trailed down from inside his hat. Something about his posture, scarecrow thin and bent from too much work, reminded Eliza of a retired gunslinger. He looked old and withered but far from harmless.

"Hell of a storm the other night," Frank said. "Thought God might just wash us all away again. Don't suppose I could claim we didn't deserve it."

He hacked, spit a glob of phlegm, and extended a hand through the open window. Bobby shook it and felt the hidden strength in the man's grip.

"Bobby Wise. This is Eliza Billings."

Eliza didn't much like him using her real name, but they'd made no agreements on aliases. When she smiled, the man's eyes widened, brightened by the sight of a pretty girl.

"It's a pleasure," Frank said. "Park it by the barn and come on up to the house."

After pulling in beside the barn, Eliza rolled the windows up and waited for Bobby to comment. He could feel her anticipation but didn't know what she wanted to hear. Their situation looked less like a threat and more like a waste of time. There was no loaner vehicle on the property at all as far as he could tell, and the idea that the man might fortify them with supplies and cash seemed ludicrous. Still, he wouldn't admit any of this. Eliza would only feel vindicated in thinking him a fool. The girl acted as if she'd been raised alongside wolves, but Bobby knew men like Cousin Frank. Resourceful sorts who'd learned long ago that moonshine, cultivating marijuana on the hillside, or turning bagman for crooked politicians was a better path through life than dying young in the boss man's coal yard. The rancher hat and slow cadence were all hiding Frank's calculations on the best ways to fleece wayward kids. If they played it cool, they'd leave with another partner and their stash further divided. If Eliza ran her mouth, they might wind up in unmarked mountain graves or fed to someone's hogs.

"It's one night," Bobby said, reading the discomfort on Eliza's face. "We'll be out of here in the morning. Be polite and we'll get out of this with minimal hurt. Understand?"

Eliza only nodded. Bobby had the gun, and that made him another man she'd survive. They climbed out of the car with Eliza carrying the books in the wicker basket. Frank stood at the foot of the porch stairs, his hands shoved into the pockets of his faded jeans. His eyes traced up her bare legs. Eliza understood that inside Frank's mind, they were engaged in unfathomably depraved acts. Her only solace was the blade hidden inside her cutoffs.

Frank reached out to take the basket from her.

"I can manage," Eliza said.

Frank stood aside and let them climb the steps. The trailer was spacious and smelled of cats. Not the ammonia reek of piss, but of dander and the musk of regurgitated wet food dried into the fibers of the few rugs tossed over the wooden floors. Eliza saw none of these cats. Probably a feral breed who'd leave dead varmints on the doorstep. They crossed the living room, with its single recliner and coffee table positioned in front of the flat screen. Frank took a few beers from the fridge and straddled a chair as he passed the cans to his visitors sitting around the kitchen table. Bobby popped the tab on his High Life and took a long pull. Eliza didn't touch hers. She worried about being considered impolite, but it felt wrong drinking in her condition.

"Ryan tells me y'all are gonna sell these books," Frank said. "Asked me to hook you up with some wheels and a place for the night. What he didn't say, and what we better work out before I extend any more hospitality, is what my cut's gonna be."

"You split the third we agreed upon with Ryan," Eliza said.

Frank took a sip of beer and looked at Bobby. "She speaks for both of you?"

"They're my books, and I'm the one who knows the buyer. That makes it my deal."

Frank nodded, a little smirk drawing up the left side of his mouth. "I suppose you think that settles it. Only it's my kitchen table you're sitting at and my roof keeping the night's rain off your head. It's my car you're gonna be taking since the one you've already got belongs to my kin. I think that gives me a few bargaining chips. I get twenty percent. That's separate from any prior deals already made with Ryan."

Eliza leaned forward for a rebuttal, but Bobby grabbed her knee under the table.

"We can do that," he said, and squeezed again, signaling for her silence. Eliza glared at him out of her peripheral vision, but she didn't protest.

"Sounds good," Frank said. "Bathroom and spare bedroom are on through the back. You might want to get washed up and lie down." He turned his attention toward Bobby. "You follow me on out to the barn. I'll show you the car."

———

The barn floor consisted of hay scattered over hard clay. Two stalls had been built in the corner for the horses, and above them, the haymow dusted the air with motes, their particles glimmering in the sunlight shining through the spaces in the wooden-slat walls. The previously smelled cats occupied the haymow. A calico and tabby-striped legion of them skulking back and forth among the shadows. Bobby couldn't hear their silent feet, but the nocturnal eyes peered down on him until the multitude's glow resembled stars at dusk.

The car Frank offered was a pearlescent Chrysler nearly two decades old. Frank leaned on the back fender and spread his arms in presentation.

"Your chariot," he said. "Inconspicuous wheels for a discreet couple on the run."

The car looked less than reliable. Only slightly better than the truck they arrived in. The rear view on the driver's side was cracked into four equally reflective quadrants, and the back taillight on the passenger side was busted. Bobby suspected the engine bore at least three hundred thousand miles. Ryan had promised fresh horsepower, not another beater on its last legs.

"I can see you're disappointed. I don't know what the boy told you, but this is the best I can do."

Bobby peered through the tinted windows. "If it runs, it'll do."

"She runs and she's legal." Frank took some bills from his jeans. "That's a little under a thousand."

Bobby didn't count the cash. Just put it into his pocket.

"Awful trusting," Frank said. He sat back on the trunk, letting the car sag underneath his weight. His muck boots swayed a few inches from the ground, stalactites of filth dripping from the heels and nearly connecting him with the earth.

"You're gonna have to get that girl on a leash," Frank said. "The way she bucked up in there. Women run their mouth, but their men reap the responsibility of the words."

"She ain't mine."

Frank nodded. "But you'd like her to be. Anyone can see that. They look like miracles until they sink you in deep water. She's got you into some deep waters, hasn't she, son?"

Bobby had spent the morning drive blaming Eliza, but now he thought it mostly his own arrogance that led him to these unfortunate circumstances. There'd been plenty of chances to walk away, yet he'd endured each escalation.

"Don't worry about me," Bobby said.

Frank smiled, showing the gap between his front teeth. "Problem is, there are things you can't resist. Things you'll have to learn from experience. Boys like you only see the allure. None of the flaws. You wanted something wild but act surprised when you get bit. You want some real advice? Wait till the little bitch is asleep and take off. Just go home. Go home and find you a little plain-Jane church mouse. The sort of girl who'll be happy with a boring boy like you. She won't mind your dull job and dull hobbies and give you a few dull kids conceived after some dull nights. Probably won't even bother to cheat. A girl like that can give you a good life. This one, she's nothing but trouble."

Frank tossed the Chrysler keys to Bobby.

"But you ain't gonna listen to me, are you?"

"Probably not."

Frank nodded. "Well, get that wheelbarrow there. It's time to feed the horses."

Bobby did as he was asked and rolled the wheelbarrow full of hay out of the barn. Outside, Frank took off his hat and knocked the brim against his knee, ridding it of the accumulated dust.

"You love the girl, don't you?"

Bobby leaned on the handles of the wheelbarrow. In the distance, the horses stalked back and forth along the fence line in anticipation. Bobby took up the weight of the wheelbarrow and moved on toward the corral.

"Heartbreak's the sort of thing you just can't defend against," Frank said. "One way or another, it's coming."

CHAPTER ELEVEN

HARLAN WINTER

The young deputy who took my statement wore a meticulously tailored uniform. He was proud of the garb, even kept the little clip-on tie most left behind in the cruiser unless accompanied by a superior. This attention to detail ended with his appearance. Terse nods punctuated each beat of my story, which he transcribed in his notebook, but the encounter was all a formality. Some senior officer must've briefed him on my history. My family's reputation went back generations in Coopersville. Two prior sheriffs had stated that countywide crime might've been cut in half had my father and uncle served longer sentences. It was a fair assessment. At one time the brothers had their hands in nearly every criminal enterprise for sixty miles around Coopersville. If you ran drugs, distilled corn liquor, or sold women, a cut of your profits paid for that pleasure. This garnered the Winter name a certain notoriety. Not to mention the things I got away with in my youth. Between familial sins and The Lighthouse incident, the law remained suspicious of any story that left me the victim.

The officer snapped pictures of the damages. When I asked about fingerprints, he informed me the department didn't have time to cross-reference half the town for a match. The idea amused me. Less than ten people a week wandered inside. Not that it mattered. I'd already wiped things down, just couldn't let him leave without acting indignant over the lack of enthusiasm. He left saying he'd reach out with any leads. The apathetic tone reassured me. I hoped the investigation would focus on the newcomer's broken window. I'd just needed to report the gun stolen in case the boy's body was ever found.

———

After showering, I changed into a fresh pair of jeans and a clean shirt. I'd managed around three hours of sleep after returning from the cemetery. No visitations from Brandon woke me. It was just my internal clock setting itself back into the sleepless routine of my country-doctor days. During The Decline, I'd been the only free source of medical care in Coopersville, and, until The Lighthouse demanded all my attention, I lived on a perpetual hoot owl shift, with hours stretching beyond the requirements of any legitimate vocation. I set broken bones, administered medications, and provided hospice care for more than a few dying men and women who had no one else. I didn't know what exactly to expect with this missing girl, but my body felt fortified for the coming hardships.

Wherever kids congregated felt like the logical starting point in my search. I lacked that knowledge, so I'd pick up Barney first. He could tell me about Eliza's frequent haunts. The truth was, I didn't know anything about kids. I'd never had a real childhood of my own. My formative years were spent like a pugilist, fighting bigger boys who wanted the renown of knocking out a Winter or simply indulging their predatory impulse by overpowering someone weaker. I took more ass whippings than I ever distributed and might've been beaten to death had my father and Uncle Abbott not trained me. We spent mornings down in the basement, working the heavy bag, a cast-off misfit one of the local gyms was throwing out until Dad claimed it for my education.

I gained some skills. The ability to regroup after taking a punch. The tenacity to continue despite my diminutive nature, which left me a scrapper often out of his weight class against the schoolyard heavyweights. Dr. McClain questioned me about this. He wanted to know where the adults were during these battles. Why had no one ever intervened on my behalf? I told him teachers were often waiting, flocking in and breaking up the combat only when things looked dire. In a strange way, letting me fight preserved my dignity. If they'd have saved me from the public beatings, I'd have received harsher punishment when the bullies ambushed me in the privacy of the woods.

Brandon became a sacrifice to my poor talents as a fighter. The harshest bullies grew tired of defeating me and simply moved on to even weaker prey. There was little sport in continuing the cycle, but a few couldn't give up the pleasure of an easy victory. Their assaults stopped only after I nearly killed Brandon. He'd been an innocent, but innocent blood was often demanded in sacrifices. The Lighthouse certainly thought so. It made me wonder about Eliza Billings. Was she an innocent, or the one holding the knife in this situation? What did that say about me if I was willing to hide a body and falsify evidence until I found her? I didn't want to consider those questions, but they rose unheeded, reminding me how easily one might slip into a legacy of degradation.

———

Barney looked as if he'd aged a decade when I arrived. His eyes had transformed into deep puckered depressions like a pair of tiny, toothless mouths beneath a wrinkled brow. He sank down in the passenger seat, and I pulled away without commenting. I let him gaze out the window for a few minutes before recounting my interview with the police. I kept the story reassuring, but I'm not sure it mattered. Barney only nodded, his mind obviously busy on the places where his daughter might've disappeared. Parental love remained a mystery to me. With no children of my own, a mother I vaguely remember, and a father granted the title only by technicality, the prospect of an actual part of your soul roaming in its own vessel felt too difficult a proposition.

"I couldn't sleep," Barney said. "I kept remembering when she was little." He looked at his lap as if expecting to find the infant from his memory cradled in his palms. "We tried hard for one, you know? Her mother had two miscarriages before Eliza and one afterward. I can't tell you the things we tried. Doctors, charms, all sorts of incantations and rituals. In the end, I'm not sure what worked. I just felt so grateful."

Barney wiped at his mouth and rubbed a wet eye. "She was so willful. Never took to our ways, but children are rebellious by nature. I always respected it, in a way. Fight the tradition, and eventually, with some age and time, she'd come back to our way of seeing the world. Now I'm not so sure."

After circling town, Barney asked me to drive by Copper Creek. He recalled Eliza saying some of the local boys camped near the shallows and spent the lazy days of summer drinking, fishing, and telling grand lies in the ways men often do when surrounded by water. I remembered the tent city that existed underneath the Sergeant William H. Campbell Bridge in the days of The Decline. Those people had all moved on, but I still struggled to associate the place with pleasure. I'd lost fingers under that bridge.

We were driving along the outskirts of Copper Creek when I saw the boy on the bike. He rode beside the shallows, the bike bouncing over sand and gravel, kicking up a gritty fog of dust.

"That's him," Barney shouted. "That's the same bike Reynolds saw."

"We'll talk to him," I said. "Keep calm or he'll bolt."

I pulled the car alongside and rolled down the window.

The boy cocked his head, no doubt confused by the sight of two strange men trying to flag him down. He pedaled faster. According to the speedometer, we were going twenty miles an hour. I could've weaved closer and let Barney swing the passenger door into him but knew the rocks would break bones and shred any exposed skin. I kept pace as the kid picked up speed, certain he'd wear down eventually.

The boy hit a rut that busted his front tire and made the bike frame shudder. The kid performed a kind of hop off the seat and let the bike drop. I expected him to run, but he only stood waiting, hands on his knees, as he huffed and panted. Barney was out of the car before I came to a complete stop. Closer, I saw the swell of the boy's fat lip and the deep split separating the flesh like half-peeled fruit. The boy drew a folding knife from his jacket pocket and exposed the blade with a flick of his wrist. He held it out, slicing the air before him in a deliberate back-and-forth.

"Stay back, fucker," he said.

The blade didn't dissuade Barney. He kept moving toward the kid, hands up in a gesture of false peace still suitable for grabbing someone by the shirt collar. I had no doubt the kid would cut him. By that time, I was out of the car and pointing the pistol at the boy. My hand trembled while my face remained stone. I'd shot men before but never pulled a gun on a kid. I choked back something rising from my sternum and forced myself to steady my aim.

"Set it down, kid. I'm not trying to hurt you. We just have a few questions."

There was a moment when I thought the boy might lunge. My finger involuntarily tightened around the trigger, and I closed my eyes, not wanting to see the bullet's impact. I took a breath, opened my eyes, and kept the gun on the boy until he dropped the knife in the dirt between his feet.

"Smart move," Barney said, and grabbed the kid by the shirt. As the fabric ripped, Barney buried the fingers of his free hand in the boy's hair. I put the pistol away. Waves of nausea surged up from my stomach until I nearly vomited. Still holding the boy by the tufts of hair, Barney bent and scooped up the knife. He pressed the blade to the child's forehead as if preparing to scalp him.

"Where's my daughter?"

"I have no idea what you are talking about," the boy said. His mouth hung slack, ragged breaths hissing between his crooked teeth.

Barney pulled one of the long locks taut and sawed at it with the knife. He dropped an inch of hair between the boy's feet. The kid began crying. Not hysterical sobs, but the quiet tears of someone hurt often and prepared to endure more pain.

I knew nothing about the desires of teenage girls, but the boy didn't seem right for Eliza. My hunch went beyond the kid's lack of attractive features. There was an underlying malevolence, a demeanor of cruelty that pulsed from the boy even as he found himself victim, waiting on the sort of punishments he'd have administered if the tables were turned. Some girls liked bad boys, but I didn't see Eliza going on midnight rides with this heathen.

"My daughter. Eliza Billings. Tell me where she is, or I start cutting more than hair. First, I'm gonna carve your nose. Next, I'll stab out an eye. Understand?"

The boy pissed himself. Urine leaked down the denim inseam. "They said they were going to Florida. They wanted a ride and some money."

"Where in Florida? Who is *they*?"

I came forward and put a hand on Barney's shoulder. "Go easy. He's talking."

But Barney refused to lower the blade. "Who is *they*?" he repeated.

125

"Her and Bobby. Bobby Wise. She had a buyer for some books. I gave them our truck in exchange for a cut of the profits."

Barney lowered the knife. Something about the last comment had turned his fury into bewilderment. I watched him consider the testimony, still holding the boy by the hair.

"And the bike?" Barney asked. "Where'd you get the bike?"

"Bobby owed me the bike."

"Tell me about the truck you gave them."

The boy related the make, model, and color. He even rattled off the license plate.

"Did they tell you the buyer's name?" Barney asked.

"That's everything," the boy said. "I swear to God."

Barney released him. The boy took a few steps back until he was out of Barney's reach. There was no shame over his wet pants and a surprising lack of hysteria. I'd expected him to rant, curse us and offer threats of revenge, but the boy just assessed the injuries to his scalp. He rubbed the chopped patch and scowled.

"Can I have my knife back?" he asked.

Barney scoffed. "I know you're the toughest piece of trailer trash around, but if I find out you've lied about my daughter, I'm coming back and cutting your little nuts off."

The boy spit a glob of blood. The cut on his lip had reopened during the struggle.

"Fuck you, witch." He pointed a finger at me. "You, too, you bitch. How tough are you without that gun?"

Regardless of the beating, my pride always forced me to stand back up rather than stay down. Like this kid, I cut with my words, dismantling enemies with a sharp tongue whenever my fists proved inadequate. There were always repercussions, but that pain was nowhere near the trauma I'd endure if I didn't say my piece. This boy was the same. If we lingered a minute longer, he'd work up more blood to spit in Barney's eye.

"Go on," Barney said. He pointed upstream with the closed blade. "Get out of here."

We watched the boy walk the bike along the shore for a long while before piling back into the car.

———

We couldn't go back to Barney's after the way I'd terrorized Reynolds. I was only wasting gas, so I drove downtown and parked across the street from one of the little bistros where the newcomers sat outside eating brunch. We watched the young couples dining. Men dressed in chinos and linen shirts with their beards trimmed down to stubble. The women sipping sweetened coffee from white china mugs, large sunglasses shielding their eyes against the valley's remaining hours of daylight. I envied their leisure. The men, their easy lives and hands that never ached from work or fights. The women, their beauty and how they shared it with men I considered unworthy. Not that I was more deserving. Since we'd left Copper Creek, I kept thinking about pulling the gun on that boy and standing idle while Barney sheared him with the knife. The moment mirrored too many other events from my life, times when I'd followed others into violence with a willingness I kept hoping to abandon but found myself unable to change. After so many repetitions and so many opportunities for even the subtlest alteration, I had to admit that not much had changed since I'd beaten Brandon with the lock. Not even his reminder was enough to dissuade me. The truth was, the single ghost remained a lesser sentence. I was getting off easy compared to the constant procession of spirits that might've followed as a reminder of my sins.

"You think I was excessive with the boy?" Barney asked.

"Your actions aren't my responsibility. I'm angry at myself for putting the gun on him."

Barney nodded. "You wouldn't have used it."

"I might've, if he came at you with the blade."

"Pretty hard to feel sorry for someone who would've stuck me for my watch under different circumstances. How can they be so young and already predators?"

I kept thinking about Barney's trailer park insult. He never considered the true circumstances of the kid. All he saw was a broken thing better put down than rehabilitated. Like the couples dining across the street, Barney wanted Coopersville swept clean. Burn the trailer parks and starve out the food stamp recipients; then you could buy the real estate cheap, build strip malls and cafés with outdoor seating in the mountain air without looking at the people who once inhabited these hills. Ironic opinions, considering the cities these outsiders had been exiled from were built by our toil, the skeletons of their towers forged with the coal beneath our feet, and the endless sea of lights in their brilliant skylines kept burning by that same stone for which men sacrificed their lungs and lives.

Maybe the other newcomers considered Barney a misfit, but that didn't make him my ally. I was nothing more than a hired hand, and he was just another boss. All I wanted were my books back.

"You knew the buyer as soon as the boy mentioned Florida," I said. "Don't deny it."

"His name is Douglas Clark. He's a dangerous man."

Even after his performance with the knife, I suspected our interpretations of *dangerous* might be different. After all, Barney hadn't grown up with the same men as me.

"I used to call him 'the baffled king' behind his back. A spoiled old man slumming in magic circles out of boredom and lack of a real personality. That was my earliest impression. I was wrong. Compared to Clark, things like my little coven and podcast are laughable. He's a seeker of much darker stuff."

"Be specific."

"Here's a story. Clark found himself competing against these two men, the Rulfo brothers. Nothing serious in the beginning. The brothers outbid him on books at auctions, or they'd scoop up a piece of antiquity Clark was interested in. Simple stuff, but Clark holds a grudge. It vexed him. One day the younger Rulfo brother just falls over dead in the sauna after his workout. The doctor says he threw a blood clot and suffered a massive embolism. The day of the funeral, Clark arrives with condolences and flowers. The older brother thinks he's ready to end the rivalry until Clark shows off a new piece of jewelry. A gold bracelet with three pearl-shaped pieces of ivory. At least, that's what the older brother assumes, but Clark informs him the pieces aren't ivory at all. They're his little brother's teeth. Clark says now that he possesses the teeth, he holds the brother's soul inside the charm."

I'd heard similar rumors spread so the superstitious grew fearful, lies that ensured Clark wasn't outbid anymore at auction. Occult circles operate on reputation and clout, trying to convince someone you maintained a power they didn't possess. It was the same kind of mindfuck that made me question whether Barney's coven really saw Brandon's ghost at dinner. Persuade someone you have an ability they lack, and you can make them do most anything.

"How would he get the teeth?" I asked.

"There's no way to be certain if it was real, but I believe Clark could manage to have a few teeth extracted before the cremation."

Barney glanced at himself in the rearview mirror and poked at the puffed skin under his eyes while searching for the words to continue.

"People are divided on this kind of magic. Hell, people are divided on the idea of a soul, but this drives the older brother crazy. He obsesses about releasing his younger brother's spirit from Clark's prison. He tries a thousand spells of his own but can't be sure. He needs a sign, something to let him know his brother is truly free. Eventually he goes to Clark and begs.

He promises him he'll give him anything. Clark offers the older brother a trade. He can have the charm with his brother's teeth. All he wants in return is the older brother's right ear. Story goes, Clark took it off with a razor."

"You'll do a lot for family," I said.

"Anyway, that's not how the story ends. The older brother goes home and locks himself in his study. He never comes out. Doesn't eat. Doesn't sleep. Just searches his books for some kind of way to save their souls from Clark. In the end, he died a year to the day from his younger brother. The housekeeper found him in his favorite chair, the door locked and no signs of foul play. His heart just gave out. Something hereditary."

I waited on the conclusion. The moment where the hook-handed killer or whatever other concocted vestige of urban legend rose into the story's light.

"When they buried the older brother, he was missing the same three teeth."

"And you believe this horseshit?" I asked. "It's the kind of boogey-man legend people in our circles love. A rumor that keeps people from fucking with the wrong guy."

I could just imagine Barney recounting the story on his podcast, milking the five-minute anecdote into a multiple-hour discussion with new guests coming on each episode to debate the merits of the tale. Each detail scrutinized. Each plot point endlessly rehashed the same way he wanted to exploit my ghost. What I couldn't decide was whether or not it was all opportunistic hucksterism or if he actually believed these things.

Barney nodded. "You're not wrong for thinking that. I've heard a million of the same self-made legends from wannabes. Years after the rumors of his war with the Rulfo brothers, Clark showed me his collection. I held that ear. It was warm, like the man was still alive."

Across the street, waitresses in white blouses and black slacks collected credit cards and cash tips left on the table. Dusk would be making its early arrival in the valley. Barney took a deep breath and held it, released it in a slow, soundless whistle of pursed lips.

"I have to find Eliza before she gets there. Clark wouldn't hesitate to hurt her. Not after the things I've done to him."

Barney didn't recount these offenses, but they would come eventually. There were a lot of miles between here and Florida. I'd hear it in an airport lounge or roadside motel. The story needed recited at night like a bedtime prayer.

"So do we drive to Charleston and book a flight?" I asked.

"She's got a good head start," Barney said. "If we take turns driving, we can make it by tomorrow morning."

CHAPTER TWELVE

ELIZA BILLINGS

Cousin Frank put them up in the spare bedroom in back. Bobby warned Eliza about his condition, apologizing prematurely for the inconvenience, but she still wasn't prepared for the sounds the boy made. He was asleep within minutes of lying on the pallet of quilts and blankets spread across the floor, and Eliza listened to him snore and strangle, his breath catching in hitches that made his body shudder as he gasped. It was like watching a man drown in the open air. Bobby expired and was continually resurrected throughout the night. Somehow this cycle never woke him. Eliza listened for hours. She thought exhaustion would overwhelm her, but every time sleep approached, a particularly devastating attack stole the boy's oxygen. Eventually she climbed out of bed and, moving carefully not to step on Bobby, walked to the bathroom. Eliza pissed without flushing. She didn't want to wake Frank.

She washed her hands under a leaking drip from the faucet and dried them on her sweats since there was no hand towel. When Eliza stepped into the kitchen for a glass of water, Frank was sitting at the table. He wore a white T-shirt with the neck stretched out of shape and sweatpants cut off into shorts. A six-pack of beer sat in front of him. Ashes and a few cigarette butts filled one of the empty bottles. Frank had another smoke lit, its cherry glowing in the kitchen's darkness.

"Couldn't sleep?" Frank asked.

"Can you hear him?"

"I dated a girl with the same issue once. Nothing as serious as that boy, but she wore the flight mask at night."

Frank took a drag and sipped his beer before exhaling the smoke. Eliza understood the juvenile trick was meant to impress her, so she smiled as scripted. Frank pushed out the chair across from him with his bare toes and gestured for her to sit. The intensity in his stare unnerved her. His eyes never blinked, as if the man refused to miss a moment.

"Want a beer?" he asked.

"No, thank you," she said.

Frank took another drag. "Cigarette?"

Eliza shook her head, and Frank smiled around the Kool clenched in his teeth. "No vices at all, I suppose? Makes me wonder how you got into this situation. That boy in there, he ain't your man?"

"I don't have a man," Eliza said.

"I'm sure you know how he feels. Girls always know."

Eliza shifted in her chair, trying not to telegraph her discomfort. A couple hundred miles away from home in a stolen car, and now here she sat in a stranger's kitchen, the blade she'd smuggled for protection left under her pillow because she'd been scared of the boy instead of the wolf waiting in the other room. There was a knife block on the kitchen counter behind her, but that twelve feet or so between the counter and the table felt like an unbreachable ocean.

"Is he the father?" Frank asked.

Of course he'd known. If a wolf could smell blood, surely he could smell the lack of it. Eliza crossed her legs but thought better of it and uncrossed them. She needed to be ready to run if Frank moved on her. No indication of that yet. He sat still as a shadow, those unwavering eyes watching her.

"Gonna answer my question?" Frank asked.

"He's not the father."

"Didn't seem like the kind you'd give it up to, but you never know. I'm assuming that means he doesn't matter to you?" Frank didn't wait on a response, just paused long enough to ash his cigarette. "Why don't we make a deal? You leave the books with me. I'll let you walk out of here. I'll take care of the boy. You just take the truck and go on down the trail. Otherwise, I'll bury both of you in the soil behind the barn."

Eliza couldn't breathe, the scream she'd been building silenced in her frozen chest. Only a tremble traveled across her shoulders, shaking her until the chair creaked.

Frank hit her in the side of the head with his open palm. The blow knocked her off the chair onto the floor. He was upon her immediately, hands gripping her throat, relinquishing the hold on her neck only long enough to tear at her clothing. Eliza tried curling up into a ball, but the man was too large, able to pry her hands from her face and smack her again. She scratched him, raking deep with her nails until his cheeks welled with blood. One of the beer bottles had fallen off the table. It lay sideways, the last drink soaking into a discarded cigarette butt that floated inside. Eliza managed to get her hand around the long bottleneck and shattered it over Frank's head, spilling the dregs of beer and wet ash upon her. Frank sagged from the blow, a widow's peak of blood tracing down his forehead as Eliza smashed the broken bottle against the man's right ear. Frank fell over on top of her. Eliza slid out from under him and grabbed one of the knives from the block. As Frank rose up on his knees, Eliza buried the blade to the hilt just above his collarbone where the black plastic handle jutted out from the seeping skin. Frank put a hand around it, ready to pull the blade free, but thought better of it. He sat down with his back resting against the kitchen cabinets underneath the sink.

When Eliza turned away, she saw Bobby standing by the kitchen table. They watched as Frank opened his mouth, but only blood trickled out. Eliza supposed he must be choking on it, drowning in the flow she'd created. He gagged hard against the tide, and Eliza heard his gurgle, a thick syrupy sound, before the unblinking eyes went dark. They never shut. Not even for the briefest moment.

"Are you okay?" Bobby asked.

Eliza crossed her arms over her chest, securing her torn shirt. An arterial spray had cascaded over her neck and legs. She felt the warmth of the blood and understood that it was Frank's last warmth. Searching herself, Eliza realized she felt absolutely no guilt. Given the chance, she'd have killed the bastard twice. Bobby stepped around the body and helped her up off the floor.

"Go get cleaned up and change," he said. "I'll take care of this."

Eliza staggered to the bedroom, grabbed her jeans and the dirty T-shirt from the day's drive. She needed fresher clothes but couldn't imagine wearing something of Frank's. She went to the bathroom, aware of the sounds of Bobby searching the house. The shower seemed lukewarm after the blood, but Eliza stayed underneath the spray and watched the pink water circle down the drain. Two bodies in forty-eight hours. She didn't see any way out now. No self-defense claim could be made that wouldn't require the whole story. Eliza pushed all thoughts away. Just keep moving. Scrub away the blood and move on to Mr. Clark's.

When she returned to the kitchen, Bobby was waiting at the table. A few plastic grocery bags stuffed with their stolen books and other supplies rested in a chair. A hint of smoke filled her nostrils. A smell in the air like burned fried chicken. Bobby had set a large pot of oil boiling on the stovetop. In minutes, it would be a plume of flame.

Bobby had taken the knife out of Frank. It lay washed on the table, and Eliza wondered if it would be better to take the murder weapon with them or place it back in the block as if she'd never touched it. The fire Bobby set in motion would reduce the body down to charred bones. It wouldn't hide their crime but might destroy enough clues to conceal the identity of the perpetrators. Was she a perpetrator? If not damned for this body, what about the prior one they'd left behind?

Bobby took her by the shoulders and led her out the door. The house was glowing through the front windows by the time they reached the barn. The horses were scared, whinnying and restless in their stalls. Bobby petted their noses and flanks. The animals calmed a little, stopped their stomping and snorting as Bobby opened the barn and led them out into the night. Eliza watched from the passenger seat of the car.

Bobby looked brilliant in the firelight, standing between the two horses as he removed their bridles. Eliza thought she was seeing the best possible version of Bobby. No matter how many years of accomplishments or trials, he might never have another second as solidified in promise as this moment, comforting horses while a traumatized girl watched him through the hay-darkened windshield. Eliza wished he'd return so that she could tell him, but he stayed with the horses, tending to their needs as he'd tended to her own before coming back to the car. When he arrived, the thought was gone. She was back to being cold and scared, wanting only the road and the distance between themselves and this fire.

———

He didn't ask her about it until they reached Florida. Something about the rising sun and sweltering heat across that imaginary line must've given him bravery. They weren't silent the whole way. Bobby spoke a little, checking to see if she was wounded beyond the slaps he'd seen her receive. Eliza didn't respond with words. Just answered these inquiries with a nod or shake of her head. Her jaw ached. In the rearview, she could see the swelling around her left eye. The way the drooping lid threatened to close. At one point Bobby reached over and took her hand like he'd done in the tunnel.

"You had to do it," he said.

What a stupid thing to say. She'd never contemplated anything different and knew this was only substitution for the other thing he really wanted to tell her. The real questions he wanted to ask and that she didn't want to answer.

"You did a good job with the horses," she said.

"My grandfather had an old mare named Sally. She was too elderly to ride, but he'd let me feed and brush her when I visited. Papaw kept little apples in his coat, and Sally would follow him around. He taught me to do the same thing so she'd like me. That horse was my first friend."

Bobby was still holding her hand. Eliza could almost read his thoughts of their imagined life together. The fantasy of putting these miles and violence behind them and moving somewhere distant, either a foreign beach where the taste of salt greeted you with the morning wind or a frozen northern mountain where Bobby would split firewood to fight the cold nights. She knew he imagined them growing old without the strife of ordinary life: no fights over whose turn it was to wash the dishes, no woes over money, and no jealousy because of the way another man looked at her during a party. A perfect storybook love that couldn't be altered by time or deceit or the intrusions of others. Eliza understood it was her job to kill this dream.

"How much did you hear?" she asked.

Bobby gripped her hand tighter. "I heard enough."

"None of that vague bullshit. How much?"

"All of it." He was silent for a moment. "I don't understand why you couldn't tell your father."

"He'd have made me keep it. I'm not doing that."

"And I killed the father?" Bobby asked. "I guess a part of you hates me for that."

"You didn't mean it." But a part of her thought Bobby might be right. *Hate* wasn't the proper word. It was more a feeling of resentment.

A pitying frustration that despite all that had transpired, he still held her hand with a conviction she'd never known from another, and the truth was, she felt unworthy of such devotion. She neither wanted nor deserved it. Not from Bobby. Not from anyone. She let go of his hand, breaking the seal of their combined sweat.

CHAPTER THIRTEEN

ELIZA BILLINGS AND BOBBY WISE

Clark's estate didn't sit on the coast, as Bobby anticipated, but lay farther inland, hidden deep within a secluded acreage of pine, oak, and
ash. The proximity to Jacksonville should've given Gladwell substance,
but the town felt like nothing more than a forgotten outpost hewed out
of the wilderness. Eliza found it remarkable how similar the place was
to Bluebird. No tourists on the quiet streets and no migration of the
beach culture inland. This was not the sun-golden tropics of their fan-
tasies. Not a land of sugar-white sand and citrus, but a barren expanse
that would render no new terrain other than swamp. Bobby looked
particularly disappointed. He rolled the windows down in the stale
heat, casting sorrowful glances as if he'd expected beauties in bikinis to
meet them at the state line.

"How far are we from the ocean?" he asked.

"You're forty miles from the coast. The whole state isn't beachfront
property."

Even if the boy had never seen the ocean, Eliza couldn't keep the scold from her response. This odyssey was only another mistake. A cursed journey where all these foolish ideas of salvation proved fruitless. Something masochistic wanted her to go home and face the consequences. Her father would find a way to save her from the murders, but motherhood and a life devoted to the coven was its own kind of atonement. Bobby's freedom kept her pressing on.

Clark's turn-of-the-century manor would've shamed any neighboring mansions had it been built in the suburbs instead of the sticks. Bay windows faced outward from the sun-bleached red bricks, and a tower that accentuated the tiled roof crested against the horizon. Bobby parked the car in the shade underneath two live oaks and a golden rain tree. A man too young to be Mr. Clark watched them from the porch. He stood by the front door with his hands in the pockets of his slacks and a cigarette dangling from the corner of his mouth. The man didn't greet them as they exited the car. He waited until they were almost to the porch before speaking.

"Can I help you?" he asked. His voice was thick from smoke.

"We came to see Mr. Clark," Eliza said.

"This is private property. I'm afraid you'll have to go."

"Tell him it's Eliza Billings and that I have some books for him. He'll want to see me."

The man flicked his cigarette away. "Wait here," he said.

They stood waiting, both silent for what seemed like a long time, until the man came back outside and welcomed them into the house. Eliza expected their meeting with Clark to take place in the den or another of the many rooms meant for entertaining, but the man led them through the living room toward the back of the house. They stopped at a small alcove with large double doors at the end of the hall. The man gestured them into a spacious office, where a pair of wingback chairs sat before a long polished desk. Mr. Clark sat behind this desk, wearing a dark suit and tie as if waiting to receive company. He was a small man with a forgettable face partially concealed by a closely cropped beard. His hair was thick and too long. Traces of stark white streaked through the combed part and around his temples. Eliza couldn't stop looking at Clark's eyes. They oscillated between a deep green or hazel, depending on the angle.

"Do you remember me?" Clark asked. He paid no attention whatsoever to Bobby but spoke to Eliza as if they were alone in the room.

"Not really. I've just heard my father mention you."

Clark nodded. "I haven't seen you since you were eight years old. That was also the last time I saw your father. What has he told you about me?"

"Nothing directly."

"There's very little about me Barney would say aloud and even less he'd allow said in your presence. You can't know much about my reputation."

Not a hint of the braggart in his statements. More the cold inquiry of a teacher testing a student's knowledge. Whether Eliza was aware of his reputation or ignorant, the truth of it would remain the same.

"I know you buy books," Eliza said.

The walls behind Clark's desk were composed entirely of bookshelves. Nothing concerning the occult or magic, just a display of modern literature in handsome clothbound first editions. Eliza did notice a copy of *Lonesome Dove*, but it and these others were nothing more than window dressing. Artful displays for guests. The real collection would be hidden away. Clark looked at the books sitting on Eliza's lap but didn't ask to see them.

"You and this boy came a long way, obviously without your father's permission, in the hopes I'd purchase your books?"

Eliza had been aware of the danger in possessing something of value since before Cousin Frank's. She'd understood greed and violence but had never encountered it. Now, sitting before Clark, she could feel the man's control over them. Her future lay in his hands. Whether he paid them for the volumes or simply claimed the texts by force would decide her fate. Worse, no sales pitch or sob story would offer any leverage. Clark could do what he willed, and Eliza knew she'd accept it the way one accepts the forward march of time. She hoped he'd deal fairly with them, but decency in others remained as arbitrary as a coin toss.

"If you don't want the books, we'll be on our way," Bobby said.

Clark let his eyes settle on the boy.

"He's tired," Eliza said. "It's been a long trip."

Clark spoke without turning to her. "I'd like your friend to wait outside with Terrance. If I'm interested in the books, you and I will negotiate a price. Those are my terms."

"We accept," Eliza said.

Terrance entered without announcement. He stood by Bobby's chair, waited on the boy to rise, and escorted him from the room. As they left, Bobby cast a look over his shoulder at Eliza.

"I'll be right outside," he told her. The statement was an oath.

Alone, Eliza waited for Clark to take one of the books. When he didn't, she set the first of them on the table. Clark turned the pages with the intensity of a man appraising a precious stone.

"Who did you steal these from?" Clark asked. He silenced her unspoken lie with a raised hand. His fingers were exceptionally long. Elegant like those of a pianist.

"The owner of these books wouldn't part with them willingly. Be honest, or our business is over."

"We robbed a bookstore. The man who owns it had these in his private collection."

Clark raised an eyebrow, but not in judgment. "Did you hurt anyone during your robbery?"

"No."

"Maybe that boy hurt someone for you. You know he loves you. Do you feel the same?"

Whenever she thought about love, panic surged through Eliza as if a doctor were diagnosing her with something terminal. Love felt like a disease you contracted, like a parasitic growth that needed removal if she ever hoped to regain control over her body. Worse, Clark asked the question as if he already knew the answer. As if the absence of her love revealed something equally broken within her.

"I don't love him," she said.

"And how does it feel to be the object of unrequited love?"

Eliza expected the answers to come easily. It might be hard to articulate, her testimony some confused musing about the embarrassment of being desired or the frustration of knowing that she couldn't make Bobby see all the flaws that marked her as unworthy, but investigating her feelings, Eliza knew all these explanations were the false statements of a coward who lacked the resolve to tell the deeper, darker reality.

"It feels like I'm stronger than him."

Clark closed the book.

"You and I have more to discuss. Afterwards, Terrance will show you to a room. It's been a long drive, and you must be tired. You'll have my answer about the books tonight."

CHAPTER FOURTEEN

BOBBY WISE

Sitting in the foyer under Terrance's guard, Bobby believed The Flinch might've finally disappeared. Eliza had been alone with Clark for nearly ten minutes. Normally a meeting of that duration would've plunged The Flinch into a panicked diatribe, yet Bobby's wait remained serene, if a little lonesome. The internal silence felt as if his last remaining friend had abandoned him. The Flinch was a burden, but with it gone, he wasn't the same. Would Eliza see the change in him as easily as he felt it, or did it take time to recognize the transformation? Probably the latter. Change meant letting an aspect of yourself die so that something new might grow in the absence. Bobby just hoped that some undefined characteristic, something as tangible as a scent, would intrigue her. He wanted time to show Eliza the better man he was becoming.

Bobby considered this until Eliza returned to the foyer. She didn't look particularly frightened, just stood at the entrance of the room while Bobby waited on an explanation.

"He wants to see you," she said.

Bobby wanted to ask what they'd discussed, but Terrance didn't allow it. He never touched Bobby, only stood beside his chair until the boy rose and let himself be led out of the room. Eliza took Bobby's hand, giving his fingertips a brief squeeze as he passed by. Bobby wished he could embrace the girl, pull her forward into the promised kiss he'd denied himself for the third time, but the moment was already gone.

After turning another corner in what felt like a labyrinth, Terrance opened a door that led down a flight of stairs. Bobby smelled the basement below—traces of rotten wood, evaporated water from prior flooding, and the arid heat of all those summer days baked into the subterranean room. Pale light fluttered as if a dying fire winked in the depths.

"Down there?" Bobby asked. Terrance didn't answer. He stood a few feet from the precipice with his arms crossed.

The steps creaked as the wood bowed underneath Bobby's feet. Clark had removed his suitcoat, unbuttoned his shirt collar, and loosened his tie. The ribbon of dark silk brushed the small man's belt buckle as he stepped out from behind a table in the far corner of the room. A presentation with jars of various sizes had been spread across the tabletop. Each was filled with a brown liquid that resembled spirits. Alcohol wafted in the air, along with the effervescent perfume of rot. Bobby couldn't make out the contents at a distance, but he knew something dead floated in each of the jars.

"Did the girl tell you about our conversation?" Clark asked, but Bobby understood the man already knew the answer to this question. Clark would've never let Eliza leave the office without extracting every detail of their journey.

"I'm the killer," Bobby said. "Both the boy in the crypt and the man who gave us shelter. I hope she was clear about that."

"It's not what you did, but why," Clark said. "Eliza thinks you killed the first out of fear and everything else was done for survival. Maybe you believe that, too, but I don't think your first was an accident. I think you did it out of love."

Bobby had leveled similar accusations against himself. He hadn't premeditated the murder, but was fear really what made him pull the trigger? He'd have said yes just last night, but there was a lingering suspicion growing from his fleeting thoughts surrounding the dead boy. It wasn't that Bobby failed to mourn him. The dumb bastard deflowered his girl and ruined his life when he caught the bullet, so some resentment was to be expected. The real questions spawned from emotions Bobby didn't like admitting. There'd been satisfaction in hiding the body. Not just the appreciation for one's own life that accompanies communing with the dead, but something more sinister. A hidden glee at leaving the corpse moldering among the McCabes. Cosmic payback against the boys who'd been dealt a better hand by life.

"Does the girl know you love her?" Clark asked.

"She knows."

"And how does it feel knowing she'll never love you back?"

"That's her business. It doesn't change me."

Clark's smile revealed a legion of teeth. Each exposed tooth looked too small for his mouth, and there seemed far too many, as if the requisite number had been traded at birth for the surplus that now crowded his gums.

The cellar felt like a place of confession. While Clark offered no absolution, there was a priestly quality in the man's lack of judgment. One sensed he'd seen all manner of sins imaginable and grown tired of our capacity for debasement.

"Girls don't like me," Bobby said. "They never have."

"And so you've chosen to love a girl incapable of loving you back. You think I'm being cruel, but it's the truth. Did she love the father of her unborn child? No doubt she shed some tears, but are tears the measure of love? Did she love her own father enough to consider how her abandonment would wound him? If she never loved these men, or even the child inside her, why should she love you?"

"You can't know a person's heart after one conversation."

"Eliza and I possess knowledge you lack. We know the true purpose of love. Do you want me to enlighten you? Love is made for weakening others. Love is for removing their self-interest until they sacrifice for you. You've recognized the narcissism in the girl, and you love her still despite it. You love her because you've grown tired of living in a world where men cast off their devotion. You believe a man must make a covenant and hold to that promise. Promises are not absolved because the recipient is unworthy or ungrateful. The oath stands, and the man who swore it remains bound. That's why you killed for her."

Observing the table during Clark's soliloquy, Bobby finally discerned the contents of the nearest jar. Several human eyes floated in the amber solution. Death and the preserving liquid masked the original color of the irises. There was no telling if they'd been green, brown, or even the turquoise blue of Eliza's eyes. A few rested on the glass bottom. Others bobbed on an invisible current. Bobby counted nine harvested pairs but nineteen eyes in all. He wondered which of the trophies—for they were obviously trophies—belonged to a man or woman with a single eye.

The other jars contained body parts as well. A woman's hand floated in one of the largest like a mummified spider. Her long, unpainted nails manicured. The ring finger skinnier as if a wedding band worn in life had slimmed the digit. Another jar was full of ears so shrunken and withered they resembled slices of dried banana. The smallest jar had been filled almost entirely with teeth. Molars crested from the liquid like the exposed peaks of icebergs in a miniature sea. In another, a heart hung in stasis with the veins reaching like vines.

"You failed the most important test of manhood when you brought her here," Clark said as he took a knife from his trousers.

The blade bore a pale handle easily mistaken for ivory, but Bobby knew it to be bone. Probably the femur of some other victim.

"Her father used this very knife to cut that heart from a woman's breast. Now I could add his daughter to the collection."

Bobby understood pieces of himself were going into these jars. His eyes scooped out and ears shaved off. Perhaps even his heart would mingle in the jar next to this still twin. He didn't think he could disarm the man. Clark's stature was small, but he held the knife with the certainty of one who'd used it before.

"Do you know which animal engages in the truest expression of love? It's not a man. It's a spider. This particular arachnid gives its offspring a signal. When the newborns receive the signal, they devour their mother. The cannibalism would mean nothing if it were only an evolutionary impulse. Both the offspring and the mother are predators, but the mother stifles any urge to consume her children. She defies her true self so the babies may flourish. You aren't a spider. I can't let Eliza cannibalize you, though I've no doubt she would if the situation called for it. Instead, I'm preserving your love now. Before time and betrayal and boredom erodes it and reveals all the fissures present in the foundations."

Bobby snatched the nearest jar and threw it. Clark dodged the projectile, and it exploded against the concrete floor, the eyes rolling in all directions like billiard balls after the break. Clark stomped over the organs in his path, the jellied orbs squishing underneath his wingtips. Bobby punched him in the jaw, but the blow didn't stagger Clark. He grasped the boy by the collar and slid the knife into his belly. Bobby felt the blade twist as the warmth drained from him. A cold enveloped him, and it wasn't until Clark retracted the knife and the room's air touched those internal places within that the pain arrived. It radiated up from the wound and through his neck until his mind misfired, trying to seize the will for fighting back. Clark slipped the blade inside again.

The new incision was only inches from the last, yet Bobby felt the blade bite into something more substantial than his intestines. Blood pooled in his shoes as Clark held the back of his neck and the men rocked in a bizarre dance. A thumb caressed Bobby's hair, and he remembered holding Eliza's hand on their drive. First in the tunnel and later that night after freeing the horses during the fire. He recalled his quiet tears in the dark and how he'd wondered whether she heard the tiny sobs he suppressed deep in his throat. There'd been a fullness in him, a feeling that everything substantial might leak out if he opened his mouth to tell her. The Flinch had stopped him, kept him silent, and forced all those eulogies and promises back down. Now, as Clark slid the blade in a third time, he only wished he'd dispelled The Flinch soon enough to tell her.

CHAPTER FIFTEEN

HARLAN WINTER

We had stopped at a Burger King for a quick piss when Barney got the call. I was inside, grabbing coffees before my turn at the wheel. Black for me and cream with three sugars for Barney. The plastic lids didn't seal properly on the Styrofoam cups, so I scalded my hand as I fumbled with the door. Outside, Barney sat sideways in the driver's seat with his legs stretched out into the lot. Tears hung in the wet scruff of his beard like morning dewdrops on grass, and the rubber band around his ponytail had come undone, letting the unsecured mane drape around his shoulders. Barney looked at the phone in his hand as if no amalgamation of wiring should be able to deliver such a message.

"Clark called me," he said.

I set the cups on the hood of the car. The other patrons were watching us. Kids stared from the tinted back windows of family SUVs as the drive-through line crawled forward. A worker on smoke break pitched their unfinished cigarette and hustled back inside, afraid of being roped into our private tragedy.

"Take your time," I said.

"There isn't any fucking time. He's already got her."

The raw panic of an animal in a trap replaced Barney's reason. He languished in the seat, eyes squeezed closed against an overwhelming pain one moment and opening in frustration the next, insistent he must do something immediately rather than explain things to me, but there were too many miles between us and Eliza. I hoped his fury would outlast the coming despair. Rage would keep Barney driving all night while hopelessness left nothing but a shell.

"Less than three hundred miles. We can be there soon if we break all the traffic laws."

Barney shook his head. "He told me not to come tonight. We're expected tomorrow at three o'clock."

Inform a man you've got his daughter hostage but demand he wait nearly twenty-four hours before the proposed exchange? The cruelty surprised me.

"Does he want money?"

"No," Barney said. "He wants me."

———

I drove fifty miles before exhaustion overtook us, and we stopped at a motel just off the interstate. One of those front-entry flea traps that cost eighty dollars a night. The sort of place where you don't bother hoping for clean bed linen and the towels feel crunchy with what you pray is too much starch. This one had a pool. A few kids splashed in the green chlorinated water while their mother supervised the night swim. She only glanced up from her phone long enough to shout down unruly behavior. Teenagers occupied the deep end. The boys circled the girls like sharks and waited on the younger kids to abdicate the shallows. I wanted to sleep but wouldn't let myself until Barney closed his eyes. He sat up in one of the stiff wooden chairs, staring at the wall as if some answers might materialize on the cheap blue wallpaper.

"I need to tell you something," he said eventually. "If you're going with me, you need to hear it."

Barney took a sip of cloudy tap water from the complimentary plastic cup. His hand trembled as he drank, and water dripped onto his shirtfront. Miraculously, his polo had remained tucked in despite the hardships of our journey.

"I told you about what happened to the Rulfo brothers. What I didn't tell you was the part I played. I'm the one who pulled the younger brother's teeth. I bribed my way into the morgue and extracted them with pliers. Clark promised that if I retrieved them, he'd share books with me. I wish it ended there."

I understood what kind of secrets came next. I'd seen the same need for expiation when my uncle Abbott came home from prison. That ungovernable desire to tell someone about your sins.

"I became a sort of apprentice. Clark showed me things that I still can't explain and have never been able to replicate. For a time, it was glorious. You can't imagine just being in proximity to that sort of power."

Outside, the kids chanted singsong rhymes as they played Marco Polo. Barney took another drink. Whatever came next, he needed me to understand things had started out with the best intentions. As if caveats about purpose excused the tragic results.

"Clark became obsessed with an eighteenth-century manuscript in the private library of another collector named Bussard. He offered twice its worth, but the man wouldn't sell. I was dispatched to convince him. Bussard was accommodating, invited me to stay for dinner, but made it clear he wouldn't consider selling the book at any price. I thought at worst Clark would insist on some sort of mild retribution. Maybe arson.

After all, if Clark couldn't have the book, he'd want it destroyed out of spite. But Bussard had a wife."

Barney reached for another drink, but the glass was already empty. There was something wistful in the way he recounted the events. He sounded like a former cultist espousing the virtues of their disbanded sect or some brainwashed victim defending their captor in court.

"I thought it would be a ransom, but Clark added her heart and left hand to his collection. I don't know what happened to the rest of the body. Three months later, Bussard killed himself in grief. Clark didn't even make a bid when the estate auctioned the books. After the buyer heard the rumors, he mailed Clark the edition that started all the trouble. I was already gone. My coven moved a lot those first years until I decided it was safe. I always thought if Clark wanted me, I'd already be dead."

Brandon's ghost had materialized in the corner of the room during the confession, but Barney hadn't seen him yet. He was too lost in his memories, too terrified contemplating his daughter in the custody of a man who kept pieces of women in jars. The ghost didn't join our conversation, simply dripped blood onto the already-stained brown carpet. Visitations were like this sometimes. Less hauntings than quiet observation. In the hospital, I used to plead with Brandon for any communication beyond the vacant stare, but I'd learned to ignore these shorter intrusions. It was the lingering, the longer intervals where I thought Brandon might never depart, that made me lash out. Not that the ranting did any good. In the hospital, raving brought the orderlies with their sedatives. On the worst nights, it seemed as good a solution as any other.

Barney crushed his cup and tossed it into the nearby garbage can. There was no plastic bag in the container. I found it depressing I could notice such mundane details despite the bleeding ghost.

"I'm taking a shower," Barney said.

The ghost stood before him, but Barney gave no indication he saw it. He simply stretched, cracked his neck as if trying to shake off all those miles, and walked past Brandon's bleeding visage on his way to the bathroom. If he'd been a few inches to the left, Barney would've bumped into the ghost. Brandon had touched me on a few occasions. These tangible manifestations felt of a substance like flesh, but cold and bloodless. The skin smooth at the palms, rougher and covered in light tufts of hair on the back of the hand and wrist. How had Barney not seen him? I remembered our dinner and the way the entire table claimed they saw the ghost seated among us. Perhaps I had displayed some clue that telegraphed the moment, but how would they know about Brandon's ghost in the first place? He was the only part of my Lighthouse story I'd kept a secret. No one knew about him aside from the doctors on the hospital ward.

Blood dotted the front of Brandon's white smock. The stains often grew the longer he stayed. Some nights in the hospital, the drip from his nose accumulated until the gown's material appeared dyed red. The way he looked like another patient on the ward always made me self-conscious of my own hospital clothes. I couldn't shake the thought that perhaps I'd died and perdition had assigned uniforms.

Brandon pointed at the tabletop.

"Why don't you just speak?" I said. Maybe a little too loud, but I felt confident Barney couldn't hear with the shower running.

Brandon pointed at Barney's phone. It was plugged into the wall and charging. I picked it up.

"It's locked," I told him. Barney punched the code in countless times on our drive. I wasn't certain about the entire sequence, but I'd watched his thumb make the motions. Up and down, then left to right in the shape of a cross. It took only four tries before the phone unlocked. Behind me, the shower still hissed. Steam boiled from underneath the door.

I checked recent text messages first, scanning through normal conversations from Reynolds and a few others I didn't recognize. Afterward, I opened the email. Scrolling quickly, I saw mostly spam. Advertisements filled the inbox, along with correspondence regarding the podcast. It wasn't until I opened the contacts that I found what I was looking for. The listing simply said *DOC*, but I recognized the number and email for Dr. McClain.

I slung open the bathroom door, releasing a gust of steam, and slid across the soaked linoleum, caught the shower curtain before falling, and tore it from the cheap rings, the metal rod bending into an agitated V as Barney, slippery with soap, tried scuttling away as I reached for his throat. I grasped that long tendril of wet hair lathered into a single braid and jerked him over the lip of the tub. He slapped at me, but I was too incensed to feel the blows. I punched him in his stomach and dragged him out onto the carpet.

I hit Barney twice in the mouth before he managed any lies. Brandon watched us from the corner. I wondered if ghosts retained any memories. If the punishment inflicted on this man reminded Brandon of the distant day from his life when I'd beaten him with the combination lock, each blow robbing him of another faculty and confining his remaining time to a hospital bed. With lines like that crossed in my youth, it would've been easy to kill Barney. I wanted to drown him in the tub like a stray cat or bash his skull in with the lid from the toilet tank. Instead, I grabbed a handful of hair and pressed the phone to his nose.

"Dr. McClain is in here. I want to know everything. Don't bother lying."

Barney sputtered and coughed. Blood leaked from his nose, mirroring Brandon's permanent wound. "I paid him for your medical records."

"Why?" I put my bootheel into Barney's soggy crotch and pressed. "What did you want? Money? My books?"

"I paid McClain, and he told me about the hallucinations. I knew if the coven convinced you we saw the ghost, I'd be able to stream the exorcism on the podcast."

Brandon didn't mind being called a hallucination. The ghost only observed, eyes glazed with apathy as I threatened to crunch Billings's cock and balls.

"What tipped you that night at dinner?" I asked.

"McClain documented your state during the episodes. You've got tells. Rapid blinking, twitches around the mouth, elevated heart rate. He even showed me film from one of the sessions."

I recalled that session. We'd been sitting in his office and discussing my father's death when Brandon arrived. I tried convincing Dr. McClain the ghost was with us. Walked over and placed my hands against the dead man's chest, feeling the frozen muscle there under the thin fabric of his smock. I promised the doctor proof if he would just come over and place his hand next to mine. When he refused, I tossed the nearest chair against the wall and turned over the table between us. The orderlies pumped me full of a benzodiazepine cocktail.

I released Barney and sat on the edge of the bed, ashamed to be fooled so easily. Perhaps I really was crazy if I didn't have the ability to sniff out such a blatant con. My mind shattered from too many years of violence and guilt.

At my feet Barney rose up on his elbows. The blood mingled with the suds in his chest hair. He cupped his testicles, massaging to make sure nothing had ruptured. Brandon had disappeared sometime during the fight. His absence left me feeling alone.

I could just leave. Take the car keys and abandon Barney to the shithole room and the near-certain violence of the coming day. I thought of the trapped girl. The jars of flesh housing the heart of the collector's wife.

"Go rinse off," I said. "We need to sleep."

CHAPTER SIXTEEN

ELIZA BILLINGS

That night, Clark came to Eliza's room, carrying an oblong wooden box. It reminded her of a shoeshine kit that had belonged to her grandfather. This wood was paler, the grain smoother, and it emitted a crisp floral scent instead of the harsh odor of shoe polish that filled her grandfather's closet and always clung to the fibers of the man's shirts. Eliza didn't rise when Clark entered. She sat on the edge of the bed as he placed the box beside her atop the green duvet.

She'd been locked inside the bedroom for hours. Terrance led her upstairs under the pretense that she might rest while Clark reviewed the books, but the door was bolted once it shut behind her. After calling out and beating the heavy door, Eliza finally lay back against the bed's wrought iron headboard. Sleep wouldn't come, so she sampled the cooling tea left for her on the nightstand. It tasted of mint and eucalyptus, but a chalk undercurrent contaminated the flavor and coated her tongue. She'd grown tired and slept until Clark's intrusion.

Outside, the sun was down, and the blue glow of either dusk or approaching dawn illuminated the gossamer curtains through the window. Clark had changed out of his suit but wore another fresh white overshirt, his french cuffs secured with onyx cuff links.

"How was your rest?" he asked.

"What have you done with Bobby?"

"I have a present for you," Clark said. He removed a chair from the vanity across the room, sat down near the foot of the bed, and lifted the box onto his lap.

"A decade ago, your father asked me to share my knowledge. Back then, our relationship was transactional. He'd procured a few books for me, and I paid him well. I thought I understood what kind of man he was. Mercenaries are all the same, but he was adamant about wanting to learn. I'll admit that he intrigued me. I agreed on one condition. He'd put his hand inside this box and leave it until I gave him permission to remove it."

"What's inside?" Eliza asked.

"That's different for each person. Sometimes it's a fear. Sometimes a desire."

"What did my father feel inside?"

"Spiders."

Eliza knew spiders were the only thing her father feared. He told her it had always been that way, even when he was a little boy. Something about all the legs. The idea of being wound up in a silken knot and helplessly waiting until the monster decided to eat you. He didn't even like killing the tiny ones they found hibernating in the house during winter. Eliza spared him this duty by smashing them with a book or shoe, wrapping them up in a paper towel, and tossing them outside. Her father didn't like disposing of them in the garbage or flushing them down the toilet. Eliza imagined him sitting on the bowl, wondering if the creature might crawl up from the septic tank for revenge. Once, she'd threatened him with one of the flattened corpses, its broken legs glued to a magazine cover by guts. Her father fled upstairs like a child and locked himself in the bedroom. She never played the prank again.

"You kept spiders in the box?"

When Clark didn't answer, Eliza knew he wasn't going to explain further. She thought about her father placing his hand inside the box of spiders. Did he feel them right away? A horde crawling atop one another in the darkness. Hundreds of hairy legs tickling his palm. The thick braids of silk webbing entangling his wrist. It was a small box, but Eliza envisioned an infinite internal expanse with tarantulas the size of dinner plates. Their legs thick as licorice ropes and fangs strong enough to clip the wings off small birds. She imagined younger spiders born in that darkness and never knowing sunlight. Their only meals the flesh of weakened brethren.

"What happens if I don't do it?" she asked.

Clark only smiled, allowing her to see the way his teeth huddled together in his mouth. In some kind of orthodontic anomaly, there were no gaps or spaces whatsoever in the rows. They seemed so fused Eliza thought it would be impossible for the man to floss.

"I don't have to persuade you. You'll do it because you want to know."

Clark unclasped the brass latches and lifted the box lid in invitation. Eliza tried peering inside but saw only darkness. She closed her eyes and reached out with her right hand. At first the inside was only warmth, like submerging her hand in dishwater. As Eliza stretched her fingers, the contents became more viscous. A sticky, jellied substance coated up past her wrist. She touched the thigh first. Smooth and hairless, the skin imbued with a softness beyond anything she'd felt before. Slim as a sapling's trunk. It could've been encircled by a thumb and forefinger.

Eliza traced a line down until she felt a foot. Tiny toes wiggled in response to her touch. She thumbed over each digit and was surprised by the hardness of the toenails.

It was a boy. She could smell him in the room. The toasted-sugar scent infants gave off from the crown of their head and the base of the neck. The eyelids fluttered. Somehow Eliza knew that he would have her eyes. The child was perfect and would grow into a handsome, kind man. Her own mother had tried conceiving for years before Eliza was born. Eliza lost count of the miscarriages, and still her father continued filling her mother's womb with children doomed to never take their first breath. There were couples who prayed for nothing more than this moment, yet Eliza knew she didn't want the boy. Being a child with her own children filled her with dread. This was no epiphany, but the certainty of the conviction frightened her. She remembered Michael's obsession and Bobby's romantic overtures. The way the boys looked at her sunbathing, salivating for a peek at her eyes behind the sunglasses as if nothing in the world could be more spectacular than a hint of those turquoise irises. She recalled Bobby's hand on hers in the tunnel and the hardness inside her that couldn't be penetrated. If that devotion was the proper measure of love, Eliza didn't have enough to give.

She tried pulling her hand free, but Clark grabbed her just below the elbow.

The child started wailing. The cries pierced the room's silence as if the infant were not inside the box but sitting upon her lap. The toes melted away in her grasp, the skin turning rough as leather and flaking apart until Eliza felt the brittle skeleton underneath. In a moment she held nothing but a handful of bones like small pebbles. She searched the rest of the body, fingers ticking over the miniature slats of rib cage and up the crooked vertebrae as if grasping a stone snake.

Clark released her, and Eliza fell back onto the bed, crying. The sobs racked her body, coursing through her until she couldn't control her trembling limbs.

"Fear or desire?" Clark asked.

Eliza wanted to kill him. Sink her thumbnails in his eyes and bite out his larynx with her teeth, but Clark ran his fingers through the long strands of her hair. There was something infinitely comforting in the gesture. She felt as if she were five years old again, her father petting until she fell back asleep after a nightmare.

"I first put my hand in the box twenty-five years ago," Clark said. "I was ready for my fears. A pit of coiled snakes. Brenda Mathis telling me she'd never love me and that I'd never please a woman. I'd fortified myself for all those eventualities. I never expected my desires could be worse than anything I feared."

Clark brushed her bangs away from her eyes. Gently, he secured her chin and turned her head. Eliza observed him through the veil of tears.

"Never be afraid of what you want, and never apologize for pursuing it."

CHAPTER SEVENTEEN

HARLAN WINTER

In my family, grudges always came easier than forgiveness. My father adhered to the gospel of an eye for an eye until I thought a vendetta the only natural response to any insult. It wasn't enough to say we weren't Christians. Sunday parishioners expounding the virtue of turning the other cheek sounded weaker than pooled wax after my father finished his violent sermons, but as the burden of my grievances grew with age, I sought to understand forgiveness. Not simply ignore injustice but absolve a transgression regardless of circumstance. There were protocols in asking for forgiveness. Apologies were rendered in return for pardons received, but the dispensation of that mercy remained an abstract idea to me. Forgiveness freed you of the obsession for revenge, but how did one actually go about forgiving? What words or actions removed the hate from your heart? I needed to know that benevolence, if only to forgive my kin.

Maybe all this explains why I couldn't manage to forgive Barney. I wanted a united front before we met Mr. Clark, but resentment traveled alongside us that morning.

———

Clark's man met us at a rest stop twenty miles outside of Gladwell. He appeared tall even seated in the Mercedes, his arms corded with muscle underneath the thin fabric of his summer suit, but a tight bun of hair kept him from being the typical goon-squad cliché. Across the grass by the vending machine huts, a retired couple unloaded a pair of Boston terriers from their Volkswagen. Aside from the elderly and their dogs, we were alone. The man didn't get out of the car, its vast length one of those gunmetal shades popularized in the showrooms. Just rolled the window down.

"Mr. Clark says you leave the car here and ride with me," the man said.

"We follow you," Barney replied.

"It's not a debate."

I didn't like giving up the freedom of our wheels, but we were in no position to argue. I climbed into the back seat before Barney could protest.

Wounds from our battle still adorned Barney's face. A decent welt puffed his right eye, and a blackening bruise spread from his high cheekbone down to the tip of his earlobe as if seeking sanctuary in the line of his growing beard. I thought our escort might comment on this, but he only held out his hand like a doorman awaiting a tip. "Your weapons."

I handed over my revolver. There was still a spot of Reynolds's blood dried on the barrel's edge. The man secured the pistol in his coat.

We didn't speak on the drive. Our chauffeur offered neither conversation, the radio, or air-conditioning. Aside from reminding us of our seat belts, he only watched the rearview with a dispassionate eye. I wished for some privacy with Barney, but he sat with his head hung like a man hearing mass, too stunned for any strategizing. I wondered if the pain in his heart overcame the ache I'd given him in his trampled balls. I didn't like animosity clouding my thoughts but wasn't able to dispel that feeling of rage from when I'd found Dr. McClain in his contacts. Before that moment, he'd ridden toward danger with an ally. Afterward, I wanted only my books and a swift resolution.

The driver must've taken us in the back way because I never saw the town of Gladwell. We exited off the interstate, turned down another unoccupied road, and found ourselves surrounded by forest. Unlike my mountains, whose peaked silhouettes announced themselves, I wondered how such an expanse of wilderness appeared so fast. The trees loomed up around the car as if sprouting from hidden seedlings. These were not my woods. They contained the same oak and maple, but deeper into the coverage were flora and fauna unknown to me. Lizards who'd freeze during mountain winters performed strange ritualistic movements, bobbing up and down as colorful birds perched among them in the branches. Not quite the macaws of the islands, but more exotic than the cardinals and austere blackbirds of home. I listened for the ill subsong of crow caws, hoping for the solace of something familiar.

The house appeared in the distance. We followed the path up the slight hill and into a car park on the property. A battered Chrysler sat under the golden-leafed bough of a nearby tree. The vulgar machine was likely Eliza's transport. As soon as our driver unlocked the door, Barney sprinted across the flagstone walkway. He made a rush for the front entrance, but I intercepted him at the gate, wrapping him up in the same bear-hug restraint practiced by the orderlies.

"Not this way," I whispered into his ear.

I expected more resistance, but his struggle was no more sincere than a child's tantrum. After a moment of jerking, Barney sagged in my arms. The driver came around and opened the gate.

"If you'll follow me, Mr. Clark will receive you on the veranda."

He led us through the front door into a main hall with a cathedral ceiling. We passed beneath a crystal chandelier dangling like a uvula in a giant's maw, up a set of stairs, and down a hallway that opened onto the raised terrace. A series of circular glass tables spread out among the latticed walls overgrown in vines, and a marble-topped bar framed the supportive brick columns. Mr. Clark sat at the farthest table in back, where tea service had been prepared for three.

I've met empaths who spoke of auras, vibrations, and other conduits to the soul. I never quite understood what they meant beyond some instinctual perception. The kind of thing another might call a hunch. Before meeting Mr. Clark, I dispelled these cosmic first impressions, but a definitive difference remained between the physical body of the man and the presence that emitted from him. Before me sat a grandfather who wore his shirtsleeves down despite the heat. However, if I closed my eyes, I might've been awaiting my final judgment before the throne of an emperor.

Barney watched the old man the way one eyed a viper. Clark remained ambivalent. The reunion with the old friend of no more consequence than interruption by a beggar.

"You're looking well, Barney," Clark said after taking a sip of tea. "This must be Mr. Winter. The owner of the book that previously belonged to The Lighthouse."

Barney spoke up before I could say I wanted that book returned. "Where's Eliza? If you've hurt her, I'll break your jaw with this teapot."

"She's upstairs."

"I don't trust a word you say."

Clark rubbed a finger across the rim of his teacup. "Barney, be reasonable. If I wanted to harm the girl, she'd already be displayed tableside on a series of platters. Sit down. We've got a lot to discuss."

The driver pulled out our chairs. I took my seat across from Clark while Barney swayed on his feet, working up the composure to sit down at our table. Closer, Clark smelled of cedarwood, spearmint, and something faintly chemical. Watching him sip, I noticed the fresh manicure around the wrinkled flesh of his fingertips.

"Since you and I have older business that may take some time," Clark said to Barney, "I think it's only fair I settle things with Mr. Winter first. After all, there's no need to subject him to our problems. He wouldn't be here if it weren't for the theft of his books. Isn't that right, Mr. Winter?"

Waiting for my response, Barney dug his fingers into the white tablecloth, piling it up as he resisted the urge for violence.

"I'm more concerned about the girl and boy," I said.

"Why would you be concerned about a pair of thieves?" Clark asked. "They've done nothing but rob you."

"Because they're children."

"The boy is old enough to be a man in a number of societies, and the girl is an expectant mother. I think that's old enough for consequences."

This news shattered something in Barney. His face went slack, jaw unhinging in a shuddering tremble as he took in a slow breath.

"What girl in her circumstance would keep the news from her father?" Clark asked. "I'm not a parent, but I think your situation would cause some reflection, Barney. Do you consider your daughter's predicament another sign of your failure?"

Bloodless knuckles gripped the cloth. "I'm going to kill you," Barney told him.

"You're going to sit and obey, or I promise I'll cut the fetus out in front of you."

"What about the boy?" I asked.

"I've got no use for young thieves. The body's down in my basement. I took pity on him and left him whole for burial."

I wondered if I could smash my saucer over Clark's head and open his veins with a shard before the driver pulled my confiscated pistol. I shouldn't have cared so much. I didn't know the boy. Only something about Clark's nonchalant delivery enraged me.

"Was he the father?" Barney asked.

"He never touched her. She did weep when I showed her the body, but she cried the way a girl might cry over a dead dog."

Barney trembled after hearing of his daughter confronting a corpse, but never released his grip on the tablecloth. "I want to see her."

"First, I'll conclude my business with Mr. Winter."

Clark removed the domed lid from a silver platter on the tabletop. Underneath, banded bills lay arranged like pastries. He placed the lid to the side and plucked up one of the stacks of money.

"There's thirty thousand dollars here. I'm happy to negotiate if you think that's unreasonable, considering the damages to your business and personal inconvenience."

"Negotiate?" I asked.

"For the book, Mr. Winter. And your considerable trouble."

This was the second time I'd had life-changing money within reach. The first time, my uncle Abbott had absconded with the cash. People died while I hunted him, but monetary value meant nothing by the time my search was over. I was already under the spell of *The Conjurer's Guide*, the slow-growing obsession filling me as I considered what secrets it might hold. Now providence had come full circle, and I was being offered an obscene amount of money to part with the book. Perhaps *offered* was the wrong word. Clark said he was willing to negotiate, but there was no mistake in his intent to buy the book and the consequences of my unwillingness to sell. I could take the payoff, or I could be another dead man in the basement.

"You've got multiple priceless volumes," I countered.

Clark nodded. "True, though the others will be returned to you. I'm only interested in Pastor Logan's book. Shall we say forty thousand?"

"Am I safe asking for more?"

Clark took another drink. Not the quaint sips like before, but a long swallow that emptied the teacup.

"I'll give you sixty thousand. Any further counteroffers, I'll consider an insult."

It was more money than I could've imagined. Enough to keep the store and transform my life into anything I desired. I should've been elated, only I couldn't help thinking of Barney's stories of hearts extracted from rivals and teeth kept as charms. If Clark had gone to such extremes to acquire books from others, why not simply display me in jars?

"I don't suppose I have much choice. I wouldn't want to end up like the Rulfo brothers."

Clark's face transformed as if he'd removed a mask. "I'm surprised Barney told you about that. He acted so ashamed of his involvement."

"If the story is true, why pay me at all?" I asked. "You don't mind murdering to get what you want."

"The Rulfo brothers were given the same opportunity as you, Mr. Winter. When they refused me—quite rudely, I might add—I employed other means. I'll see that you have the full sum. For now, fill your pocket."

Reaching for the money felt like putting my hand into a fire. I slid a stack of cash into the pocket of my jeans. The brick bulged there, stretching the denim until I thought the cheap sticking might burst. I expected the driver to lead me away, but no one moved toward the table. Silence hung over us. Clark raised the lid off another platter, where a long-bladed knife with a bone handle rested. He picked it up and tested the edge with his finger. Behind me, I heard a bullet slide into a chamber but knew better than to turn.

"Now that's settled, Barney and I can get down to business."

Barney watched the knife. I knew he recognized the blade.

"What's she worth to you, Barney?" Clark asked. "A pound of flesh? An ounce of teeth? Any of those things, I imagine, but you know I'll take more than that. You know what's truly harvested by this knife."

"Let Winter take her and go," Barney said. "We'll settle up in private."

"If Mr. Winter has heard the stories, he can stay and watch. It'll be fine instruction."

The blade glinted in the sunlight like a flash of heat lightning. Barney had ceased his trembling. His body gone rigid as driftwood, palms still atop the table. There was no pleading or cries for an alternative, the only tangible fear an oily coating of perspiration that made his shirt collar stick against his neck. I looked into his eyes. Focused and full of a steadiness I thought common in witches bound for the pyre.

"Do you want to know what I told your daughter's unrequited love before I cut him?" Clark asked. "I told him the girl was a worthless claim and he'd never mine anything of substance from her heart. That's why she didn't tell you about the baby, Barney."

I waited for rebuttals and rebuke, but Barney said nothing. He took calculated breaths, anticipating the first cut.

"Shall I go get her, Barney? Do you think if she watched, she'd learn what love is?"

"This isn't about her. It's about me and you."

"I may be wielding the knife, but I'm only the instrument. Fate determined this moment on the night you took the woman. We've only been waiting for its arrival."

The driver placed Barney's hands behind his back and handcuffed them to the chair. After checking the bonds, the driver aimed my pistol at me. Clark stood and rolled up his shirtsleeves.

I told myself I'd avert my eyes before the bloodletting began. I believed these lies right up until Clark grasped Barney's right ear and lay the blade in the crease. The carving was slow and methodical. Not a quick single slice or a dull sawing. A few arching dips and pivots of the blade, and the ear came free from the skull. Barney didn't scream until Clark stepped away, holding that piece of him. The shriek that finally came was piercing, originating somewhere deeper than lungs and throat. I told myself it was only tissue, that all Clark held was an ear, but Barney squalled like some more essential element of his person were stolen.

Clark dropped the ear into his empty teacup. He grasped Barney by the chin, turned his head, and went to work on the other ear. This one took more time. Barney thrashed, his body not letting him keep the promise of resolve made by his eyes. Somehow, he stilled his tongue. No begging or betrayals that Clark harvest from me or his daughter instead. I waited for pain to override consciousness, the brain to tap out in mercy, but Barney remained present for the mutilation. He threw his head back, blood lashing across the tabletop as the second ear came off. Clark placed this in the teacup as well, the pieces garnishing the china's lip like obscene fruit.

Barney's right eye was last. I can't recount this. I watched long enough to see the knife descend. The rest I experienced with the red flare of sunlight illuminating my closed lids. It hardly mattered. I felt the pain through my ears. Saw the digging as the blade scooped Barney's eye from the socket with the retina of my mind's imagination.

With the maiming finished, Barney slumped until only the handcuffs held him upright. Blood dripped from hollows at each side of his head. I hoped he'd die but knew he was only unconscious. The driver holstered my gun and left us.

"No hospitals," said Clark. "Just get him home. He'll want to die, but remind him of the girl. He lives for her now."

Clark leaned over Barney. "You understand. Keep breathing for your daughter."

Behind me, the driver returned, pushing a wheelchair. The seat was filled with various ointments, bandages, syringes, and bottles of medication. There was even a bag of O positive for a transfusion. The remainder of my cash sat beside these items in a tight bundle.

"I'll take you to the girl while Terrance works," Clark said.

Terrance gave Barney two injections and rubbed disinfectant on his weeping holes. He was wrapping the head in gauze as we left the veranda.

———

The girl lay on the bed, likely sedated with the same drugs as her father downstairs. She wasn't what I'd expected. My imagination had built her into some kind of outlaw—tattoos, piercings, and all the other stereotypical apocrypha of the antisocial—but she was just a little girl. Weary and scared even under the narcotic influence of the sedatives.

"I'm sure you're plotting retribution," Clark said. "Maybe not today, but some night I could wake up with my house burning down around me."

"Actually, I thought I'd slip up on the property with a deer rifle. I wouldn't need to be an expert marksman to blow your brains all over the front porch."

Clark nodded. "But you want to stay alive. Besides, I'll probably be dead within a decade. You can always buy the book back then. I might even will it to you. Take the girl home and cut your losses, Mr. Winter."

Terrance appeared in the doorway behind us. He lifted the girl, cradling her like a bride on her wedding night, and carried her downstairs.

"Terrance will take you back to your car," Clark said. "If I see you again, Mr. Winter, I'm adding your remaining fingers to my collection."

———

I rode in the back seat with the girl's feet in my lap. She was still unconscious, so I checked vitals and found her pulse faint but steady. Barney sat shotgun with his face mummified underneath the bandages. Terrance had given him a transfusion before we left, but the wounds wept until that single bag of O positive didn't seem enough to replenish the flow. He was still out, head lolling until some of the seepage dripped on the leather interior.

Terrance still had my gun. He could've driven into the woods, made us kneel in a line for double-tap executions, and abandoned the bodies for the crows, but I knew we were safe when we left without the boy. If there were graves to dig, he would've planted us all in the same plot.

None of these points helped me relax. At best, I managed a state of meditative preparedness. The drive home would be hard, and the girl would ask unanswerable questions when she woke up.

When we reached the rest stop, Terrance parked on the outskirts near the abandoned semitrucks. He took my revolver from his coat, emptied the cylinder, and returned the gun.

"I'm gonna need help getting them into the car," I said.

"Fucking unbelievable," Terrance replied. We retrieved the wheelchair from the trunk, and I helped him load Barney. The man felt heavier, as if his pain had accrued mass. Terrance placed the money bag and medical supplies in Barney's lap, and we wheeled him across the parking lot to our car.

After depositing Barney in the back seat with the money, we returned to the Mercedes for the girl. As Terrance lifted her, I heard the snap of an unlocked blade. Eliza thrust the butterfly knife into Terrance's clavicle. He staggered back, one hand grasping the doorframe and the other groping at his buttoned collar. Eliza pulled the knife free as Terrance fell to his knees. I thought she might scramble away, but Eliza stabbed the blade into Terrance's left eye. He crashed face-first onto the asphalt.

The parking lot was still empty aside from three Peterbilts. I scanned for cameras. I didn't see anything but felt sure that some surveillance monitored us. I grabbed Terrance by the hair, pulled the knife free, and snapped the blade closed. I stuck it into my coat pocket alongside the gun. Eliza cowered in the back seat.

"Who are you?" she asked. Panicked eyes and gulping breath as if saved from ocean waves. "Where's my father?"

Questions I didn't have time to answer. The drugs were in the other car. Nothing to give her to calm her down and no way to prepare her for the state she'd find her father in. I could've dumped Barney bleeding onto the sidewalk and left the whole freakshow scene behind. Instead, I put out my hand as an offering.

"We have to go now," I told the girl. "I don't have time to explain. We need to get out of here."

Eliza cowered against the doorframe like a beaten dog.

"Please, you need to trust me. I'm taking you and your father home."

Cars cruised by on the interstate. Just a matter of time before someone circled into the lot and saw the carnage. I considered the gun again but knew it wouldn't work. The girl had been through too much. She'd rather be shot than follow another abuser.

Eventually, Eliza took my hand. We stepped around the blood pooling from Terrance and sprinted to the car. The sight of her father in the back seat froze her. There was an eternal second where I watched her try to process the damage. I never doubted that she recognized Barney underneath the bandages, but there was a rebellion inside that wanted this reality to be nothing more than nightmare. Some narcotic-induced hallucination that would disappear, returning her sanity and righting the world. I knew the feeling well. I spent nights with my eyes squeezed closed, praying the same prayers that Brandon's ghost might evaporate.

In the car, Eliza lay her head on her father's shoulder, expelling muffled sounds of anguish so severe there was something transcendent in their purity. The calls of "Daddy" that spilled from her mouth between sobs were more holy than any benediction.

I got behind the wheel and turned the key. The engine fired to life. Brandon's ghost stood over the dead man in the parking lot, watching our departure. I never entertained the hope that we might leave him there. I knew he'd join the rest of my passengers before we reached home.

CHAPTER EIGHTEEN

ELIZA BILLINGS

Winter checked into the motel while Eliza waited in the car. The time alone gave her an opportunity to process the situation. Bobby was dead, and her dad might not survive the night. It was hard enough looking at the blood-soaked bandages, but she couldn't help asking Winter about the wounds. Eliza thought he might lie, placate her with promises that everything would be okay. Winter didn't try any of that. He told her the full extent of her father's injuries in a slow, measured cadence. It wasn't exactly soothing, but Eliza recognized it as practiced. He'd delivered tragedy before.

"Is he going to live?" she asked as they drove toward the motel.

"I can't say for certain. I've seen people die from less, and I've seen people pull out of worse. The human body is a resilient machine. The thing that makes a difference is having something to live for."

Eliza wanted to trust Winter. He hadn't ditched her like she would've done with him. He'd even given her the knife back. Holding the blade, she'd searched for remorse and felt something worse than its absence. Terrance made the second man she'd killed, and Eliza found she was pleased to have done it. What she really wanted was to drive back to Clark's and saw his head off with the butterfly knife. Stick him down in the basement with Bobby and that horror show of eyes floating in formaldehyde-filled jars. Only she'd never go back. Eliza understood how lucky she was to have survived that place. Not many could say they'd walked through Hell and only been singed. She looked for a way to duck the blame for what had happened to Bobby and her father, but there was no way around that responsibility. The lives she'd taken were acts of self-defense, but Bobby and her father were a different matter.

Bobby's future had become entirely forfeit from the moment she feigned interest in him. When she first saw his body down in the basement, Eliza even tried telling herself this was the better alternative. The world was too harsh for such a kind boy. Better off resigning him to oblivion than let life keep taking bites out of him. Imagine her surprise when Clark's pontifications held similar opinions. Standing over the gutted boy alongside Terrance and Eliza, Clark characterized his work as a mercy. No different from euthanizing an eyeless cat or a Spartan abandoning his fragile newborn to starvation. Eliza tried sharing this worldview, but it wouldn't solidify while looking at the dead boy. For the first time, she was certain that some brittle things needed protection.

"Do you think you can love him now?" Clark had asked her in the cold basement. "It's easy to love the dead. They don't require anything. All you owe those that are gone is a reverent place in your memory. Surely you can carve out a small space in your heart for that."

But her heart had always been stonier, the soil corrupted by some inherent vice that would not allow love to grow. Eliza didn't love Bobby even now, and that made her ashamed. The boy had died for her. One could argue he'd never lived much of a life, but it was the only life afforded Bobby, and he'd sacrificed it for a girl who didn't care enough for him to cry. This finally brought tears, but whether they were for

Bobby or anguish over her own inabilities, Eliza could not say. Clark seemed to recognize this. He handed her a linen handkerchief from his coat pocket. Eliza tossed it aside on the dirty concrete and let the tears drip down her cheeks.

"I told the boy a version of love he could understand. I'll tell you another. Love is a burden. Maybe you don't want to carry the burden of this boy, but one day you'll have to choose. Carrying nothing is not a life."

The words penetrated, but Eliza hadn't given Clark the satisfaction of knowing. She spit in his face. Globules of phlegm hung off his chin and dotted his lips. Terrance lifted Eliza off her feet, carried her back upstairs, and administered the sedative.

When they finally got her father up to the room, Winter gave him two more injections and made Eliza wait in the bathroom while he changed the bandages.

"You don't need to see this," he said.

Eliza didn't argue. Only part of her wanted to look underneath, and she knew feeding that part would starve her weaker but better half. She sat on the closed toilet lid and thought about the lives she'd destroyed. It had felt so much easier to run, until she found snakes concealed in the high grass of her future. She cried a little. This time the tears fell for everyone but herself.

Winter was finished when she came out of the bathroom. Her father lay on the bed with an IV in one arm. The bag of fluids hung on the wall, secured above the window with a strip of surgical tape. Winter sat smoking at the table. It was the kind of motel where you could still smoke. The kind of motel where you can still hide in a world with no hiding places left.

"Is he going to wake up?" she asked.

"Eventually. He's on a lot of meds."

"Will the things they gave me hurt the baby?" she asked.

Winter shook his head. "No. I believe Terrance must've had some medical training. He knew what he was doing when he patched up your father."

Winter extinguished the cigarette as if suddenly remembering the dangers of secondhand smoke. "We need to talk."

Eliza took the seat across from him. She didn't know where to begin, so it surprised her when an apology spilled from her mouth. "I'm sorry we took your books."

Winter nodded. "I'm sorry they got you into so much trouble."

Eliza shook her head. "It's because I'm broken inside. I learned that when I put my hand in the box."

She knew Winter didn't know what she was talking about, but it didn't matter. Confidants don't need to comprehend, only listen. Winter understood that much as well. He never asked her to clarify her statements or provide additional details. He listened with quiet contemplation.

"I saw the boy in the crypt back home," Winter said. "Did you do that to him?"

The question wasn't without merit. After all, Winter had watched her shiv Terrance in the eye. He was entitled to some hard questions.

"I was going to disappear with the books and blame it all on Bobby. Michael just showed up. Bobby got scared, and he shot him. After we hid the body, Bobby said he was kidnapping me."

Winter scoffed. "I've seen what you do to people who kidnap you. I'm guessing you just let the boy think he was in charge while you held the leash."

"I knew he'd look out for me on the trip. I didn't mean to get him killed."

Winter didn't say anything to that. Eliza wasn't sure he believed her. She wasn't quite sure she believed herself.

"Why not just tell your father about the baby?"

"He'll want me to keep it, and I won't let another child be born into my family."

Winter lifted a bag that rested between his feet. He pulled out a brick of banded bills and placed them on the table.

"There's ten thousand dollars here. Take it. Keep moving until you find a place to settle down."

Days ago, Eliza would've held the money against her heart and thanked him the whole way out the door. Looking at the cash now, disgust churned in her stomach. The smooth bills smelled crisp and fresh like a new book, but Eliza tasted a thick murk of spoiled meat in her mouth. She looked at her father. The fresh bandages on his face were already crusting over. There would be surgeries. There would be medical bills. She thought about her child melting away in the box and her desire to be rid of him. Somehow Eliza knew it was a boy just like her father had always wanted.

"Cash doesn't have an owner or a past," Winter said. "It just buys you a new future."

"I don't deserve one."

Winter didn't protest. He only lit another cigarette. For the first time, Eliza noticed the missing fingers on his hand.

"When I was fourteen years old, I killed a boy. He laughed at me when I had trouble with the combination on my bike lock, so I beat him with it until he bled from the nose and ears. He didn't die right away. He went blind. Never spoke or walked on his own again. He died in a hospital years later. I got away with it."

With the cigarette pinched between his remaining fingers, Winter pointed toward the dark corner of the room. Even through the smoke, Eliza saw distance in Winter's eyes as he watched some presence among the cheap watercolor prints.

"You won't see him if you turn around, but that boy's standing right there. Just staring at me and bleeding."

Eliza resisted the urge to look. She didn't know how to respond to the confession. Winter didn't seem to need a response. He never questioned whether or not she believed. Her acceptance wasn't necessary. Eliza could see that all Winter required was that she understand that he believed.

"Does he say anything?" she asked.

"Not for a long time now."

"Do you talk to him?"

"I used to apologize for what I did, but we don't have anything left to say. Now we just look at each other. If I can endure that, you can make a new life after all of this."

Winter dug in his pocket and produced the car keys. He dropped them on the table alongside the money.

"The person holding the keys decides where the car goes."

Eliza closed her fist around the cool metal, the keys' teeth pricking her palm as her grip tightened.

"I'm going to go to the bathroom," Winter said. "When I come back out, I hope you'll have taken the money and decided where you want to go."

Cigarette smoke trailed behind Winter as he crossed the room. He tarried just a moment in the bathroom doorway, his back turned toward her until only the silhouette of the man remained visible in the dim portal. The door closed by inches, eclipsing the halogen bulbs until Eliza and her father were alone in the dark. Eliza watched the corner of the room for signs of Winter's ghost but found only the watercolor wildflowers and the cobwebs dangling from the ceiling. Her father's weak breath strained through the silence. Eliza went to him and held his hand. Skinny fingers intertwined, she leaned over the bed and kissed his bandaged cheek. Her father never stirred. The hiss from the showerhead broke her spell. Eliza kept waiting for her legs to carry her to the table, to take the money and place it in her pocket, but just stayed standing as the room grew warmer. A blossom of vomit creeped up from her gut, but she swallowed it back down. The heat inside the room had grown into a full-on inferno.

When the bathroom door opened, Eliza's vision clouded like staring at the smoldering embers of a fire. The painting on the wall seemed to be melting, the flowers running down in long drips to collect in pools deep as dry wells. She felt exhausted, cemetery tired, and only wanted to lie down on the carpet.

Winter stood before her in the same dirty clothes, but the man appeared changed. His beard shorn away and wet hair slicked back to reveal the small scar on his forehead.

"Decide where we're going?" he asked.

"Take us home," Eliza said.

III

BENEVOLENT GHOSTS

CHAPTER NINETEEN

HARLAN WINTER

I was having a bad day when Eliza Billings finally returned to my shop. Brandon's ghost appeared overnight and still hadn't departed with the dawn. Like usual, the specter never spoke, just quietly bled as he stalked me from room to room. I ignored him while performing my morning rituals until I nicked myself shaving. Not a bad cut, but deep enough for a slow trickle down my right cheek. I wiped the pink shaving foam away with my fingertips.

"Real blood," I said, and flicked suds at him. "Jealous?"

I rinsed my face, applied a Band-Aid from the medicine cabinet, and went downstairs with the spirit following behind. By then the visitations were so routine I'd adopted a stance of silent apathy. Nothing else seemed to work. I refused to go back to Dr. McClain after finding him in Barney's contacts, and no spell in my books guaranteed even a momentary respite from the ghost. If something can't be remedied, it must be endured. If I couldn't dispel Brandon, I'd proceed out of spite. Some days I accomplished this better than others. That morning

I struggled with the constant presence but decided there was nothing else to do aside from work.

I'd been open around an hour when Eliza came in. She looked as if she'd left adolescence behind a decade ago. Dark-rimmed eyes from sleepless nights and a sallowness in her cheeks, the only place her body refused to shed the pregnancy weight. Eliza carried the baby in one of those swaddling slings around her neck. A light rain was falling outside, so she'd draped a scarf over the child.

"I can go if I'm not supposed to be here," she said.

A tide of memories flooded in alongside her, but something about those sad midnight eyes made it impossible to send her away. Tiny murmurs emerged from underneath the shroud. Eliza bounced the child gently. She removed the scarf and wound it around her wet neck. The child remained dry, its dark hair a tangle of tight curls.

"Do you need a towel?" I asked.

"He's fine, but I do need to change a diaper."

Before I could direct her to the bathroom, Eliza lay the child on a nearby table. She whispered to the baby, performing all the actions of a good mother as she changed him, only I recognized the pantomime from a weariness in her smile. The empty gestures might've fooled others into believing she wanted to be a mother, but the obligation weighed on her. I reminded myself this was how life worked. Currents of change drifted us into unknown waters. For those of us who managed to keep our head above the rapids, the current deposited us on unanticipated shores. We ended up living for things we didn't choose. All we needed was purpose, and the specifics of that purpose didn't matter. These changes would alter Eliza, but there was still sorrow in watching her learn to love what she'd never wanted.

"How's your father?" I asked.

Three weeks after we returned, I came by the house and was greeted by Mr. Reynolds. After apologizing for my behavior on the night I invaded their home, Reynolds and I sat on the front porch, drinking lemonade. He told me Barney refused any consultation with a reconstructive surgeon. The man hid in the basement with the door bolted. Meals were left for him on the landing, the trays and dirty plates placed back outside the door in the middle of the night. Reynolds tried anticipating a schedule and catching Barney with the door unlatched. Three nights in a row, Reynolds stayed awake, watching like a disciple anticipating the stone rolling away from the tomb, but he kept falling asleep and never saw Barney deposit the tray back on his side of the door.

There were no visitors. No new podcast episodes. The only communication were scrawled inside a red notebook, where Barney wrote out requests for basic items like books, groceries, or other bathroom amenities. Reynolds kept an elaborate diary inside the notebook, detailing occurrences around the house and Eliza's progression for his friend. He wrote that he missed their conversations. He wrote that the girl hated pregnancy but that he saw quiet moments of acceptance that made him certain she'd be a fine mother. He wrote about her playing little in-utero concerts by placing headphones on the dome of her stomach. He wrote that she'd started calling the child by name. He promised to tell Barney if he'd only open the door.

I asked Reynolds if he'd ever inquired what Eliza wanted. If maybe he'd ever considered just driving her to a clinic, sitting together in the parking lot in silence if the conversation proved unspeakable, and waiting until she made her decision. Reynolds said anytime the topic of her pregnancy came up, Eliza only chastised him to mind his own business. When he suggested that Eliza talk with his wife about her condition, the girl told him she didn't need advice from someone who'd never made a sound decision their entire life. I saw him for what he was after that. A follower with an absent leader. Nothing more than an isolated prefect waiting on the return of the king.

As Reynolds sipped his lemonade with a shaking hand, I knew he'd ask me to speak with Barney.

"Maybe he'll listen to you," he said. "Maybe he'll let you in."

I didn't think I could refuse. Not after beating both men. Not after my books were the cause of all their misery. After leading me to the basement door, Reynolds knocked and called out to Barney.

"You have a visitor. It's Mr. Winter."

We waited a moment, listening to soft steps climbing the stairs. When they stopped, Reynolds left me alone. I placed my palm on the cool wood and pressed an ear to the door. I heard labored breathing and the slow shifting of weight on the creaking stairs.

"It's Harlan, Barney," I said. "I wonder if you might let me come down and speak to you?"

A lengthy silence. Finally, a response, the voice weakened by effort after the absence of speech.

"I can hear you fine, Harlan. What do you need?"

I decided to be honest. "I don't know. Reynolds asked me to speak to you. He wants you to come upstairs."

"We both know I'm not going to do that. You were there."

It felt like an accusation. "They're worried about you, Barney. Your daughter needs you. She's been through a lot. She's pregnant and scared."

"It's not safe for me to be up there."

"What do you mean?"

"I can hear him, Harlan. He whispers to me at night."

"Who whispers?" I asked, but something inside me knew the answer.

"Clark told me he made Eliza put her hand inside the box."

"What box, Barney?"

"It was full of spiders when I put my hand inside, but Clark told me Eliza felt the baby. She felt my grandson and knew she didn't want him."

Barney's weight pressed against the door as if it might embrace him. The wood moaned. He was only on the other side, but there was an endless gulf between us.

"Help her, Harlan. Help her get far away from Reynolds and the rest of us. Promise me."

"I promise," I said, but would've said anything to remove myself from his tragedy. I didn't share any of this with Reynolds, of course. I lied and told him that Barney wouldn't talk.

On my walk back home, I thought about Clark whispering mockery in the severed ear. I should've told Barney something reassuring, should've at least sympathized by explaining the way Brandon loomed over me each night—but I could close my eyes against that invasion. There was no remedy for Clark's whispers. I'd learned to live with ghosts. He'd have to learn to live with taunts and regrets.

"Do you want to hold him?" Eliza asked.

The baby was cooing in my arms before I could respond. He was solid and heavy, the sort of good-natured infant who always smiles, exposing the wet gums in his toothless little mouth. As I rocked him, spittle dotted the tiny cleft in his chin. He had the same turquoise eyes as his mother.

"I spoke with your father, but only through the door. He mentioned something about a box."

Eliza reached out and smoothed the child's hair, but the curls stayed fixed in place.

"Mr. Clark made me put my hand inside a box. Before I did it, he told me it would expose either my fears or desires. I didn't like what it showed me."

"What was that?"

Eliza shook her head. "Mr. Clark told me that love was a burden. I thought I understood that. Loving me was the worst mistake of Bobby's life, but I didn't understand that only things we value can be burdens.

Bobby would've rather been dead than the kind of boy who couldn't love anyone. That makes me ashamed."

"Your father wants you to leave. He asked me to help you."

Eliza patted the baby's stomach. "I'm not doing that."

I nodded at the boy in my arms. "You decided to bring him into the world. He deserves the best chance you can give him. Take the cash this time. Get away from all this."

Brandon stood bleeding alongside the bookshelves. As I rocked Eliza's son in my arms, I shielded the child's eyes in case the veil between the living and the dead was thinner in infancy and the boy might see him. Eliza took her son back and placed him in the sling around her neck. In that moment, I saw the woman she might've become. All those endless possibilities that were severed when she birthed the child. Some were better than this life, some much worse. I knew what would happen if I didn't convince her to take the money. Reynolds wouldn't press, just offer invitations to study the grimoires with him or maybe use his wife to suggest the occasional protection spell for the child's health. Before long, Eliza's resolve would cave. Mother and child would be initiated into the coven she'd fought so hard to escape. Eventually, she wouldn't even remember the girl who'd tried ending that cycle.

"Just wait here," I told her, and went for the money.

Stuffing the bills into a book bag, I recalled the first person I'd ever saved before my doctor or detective days. It was on a night out at the lake with Sarah Gordon, a girl I never saw again after she transferred to another school senior year. That evening, she'd been stoned and sad, crying on my shoulder about how Debbie O'Neill told the other girls on the cheerleading squad Sarah had been talking shit about Debbie's daddy, spreading rumors of his nights out at the local parlors of sin, how he'd slink home in the early hours after his buzz finally ebbed away. They'd been nasty in that way only sixteen-year-old girls can be. Sarah was physically intact but appeared torn to shreds. Standing beside the placid waters, I asked her if she'd really said all those things.

"Well, yeah, but I didn't mean it that way," she'd said. "I just understand what it's like having no dad around."

Eventually, Sarah wanted to die. She filled the pockets of her dress with stones, placed big slabs into her leggings that ripped the tight fabric. I remember her shambling toward the shore, a boulder hugged to her chest like some prehistoric shield. She wanted to sink to the bottom, to be one of those mythical ladies in the lake whom teenagers fear when they paddle out to screw in rowboats on moonless nights.

I got my hands on her before she was too deep. Both of us stood like parishioners ready for baptism as she told me to just let her die. Instead, I carried her out before she walked far enough to wet the tips of her long hair.

"Why'd you help me?" she asked one night on the phone. I was back home in Coopersville, calling her in search of answers after Gabrielle had left me and I dropped out of school. Her voice was different after so many years. Cigarette smooth and so creamy with age that it could be another woman. In a way, she was.

"I just did what I was supposed to do," I told her.

She laughed that hoarse, mentholated laugh. "Bullshit. You have something against heroics? Did you decide a man can either be good or interesting?" She was always saying shit like that. Probably the same sort of drama that made her want to perish like Virginia Woolf.

"You weren't serious anyway," I told her, but that was a lie. I've just manipulated so many facts over the years to make reality into a more palatable fiction that truth has no distinct meaning anymore. I knew Sarah's resolve that night as we stood in the shallows and she whispered in my ear. Recalling her words, I decided to steal them to convince Eliza of the new role she might play in her father's life. Strange how a suicidal teenager's witticism might show her the instructional power the lost can impart on their loved ones left behind. Still, I knew these words would work. Years later, there was something still dangerous and alluring about them. Something that almost let me follow Sarah out into the dark water.

"We're too good for this world," she'd said, touching my cheek. A lonely siren begging me to accompany her into the depths. "Leave it all behind you. Let's be benevolent ghosts."

ACKNOWLEDGMENTS

Each book I've been privileged enough to write owes a great debt of gratitude to the many people who've made my artistic life possible. The following list expresses my appreciation for those individuals. I wish this gesture represented my true level of thanks, but words can only do so much.

First, my incredible agent, Noah Ballard, is the best partner I could have in this business. Thank you for being such a valuable adviser, advocate, and friend, Noah. My sincere thanks to my brilliant editor, Megha Parekh, for believing in this book series. My thanks to Megha, Clarence Haynes, Miranda Gardner, and everyone at Thomas & Mercer for their support of my writing.

My thanks to the teachers, workshop members, writing mentors, and other writers who have supported my work over the years, including Belinda Acosta, Jonis Agee, Nathan Ballingrud, Joy Castro, Sean Doolittle, Megan Gannon, Smith Henderson, Gabriel Houck, Ted Kooser, John Van Kirk, James A. McLaughlin, Devin Murphy, Bernice Olivas, Raul Palma, Rachel and Joel Peckham, Casey Pycior, Ron Rash, Timothy Schaffert, Bradford Tatum, Chris Harding Thornton, Anthony Viola, Stacey Waite, Nick White, and John Woods.

My thanks to my family and loved ones. I hope to keep making you all proud.

Finally, my love and thanks to Ashley. Your love is the greatest gift I could ever receive. Thank you for making me a better man.

ABOUT THE AUTHOR

Photo © 2022 Raphael Barker

Jordan Farmer is the author of *Lighthouse Burning*, *The Poison Flood*, and *The Pallbearer*. He was born and raised in a small West Virginia town, population approximately two thousand. He earned his MA from Marshall University and his PhD at the University of Nebraska–Lincoln. For more information, visit jordanfarmerauthor.com or follow @JordanFarmerPhD on X (formerly Twitter).